Legerdemainia

Legerdemainia

by

Ron Sanders

ISBN: 978-0-6151-8238-4

other works by this author:

Freak

Signature

Microcosmia

Carnival

The Deep End

Moth In The Fist

Hero

ronsandersatwork.com

ronsandersartofprose@yahoo.com

Legerdemainia

The Fartian Chronicles

Sympaticus

Mondays are always the worst.

In any occupation, white collar or blue, starting the work week means dying anew. Those urgently needed extra hours seemed only to rip off Saturday morning, and Sunday, far from being a day of rest, quickly became a grueling countdown to tomorrow. Weekends are over before they begin.

And for Fartian counselors beginning a new week at the Bureau of Terran Grievances, Monday's just the first bump in a long slide to nowhere.

The waiting room is always full, the clientele never pleased. After courteously blowing their minds trying to figure who should get to watch what, Fartians had magnanimously overhauled the entire building, adding sets, satellite dishes, and routers, so each Earthling could channel-surf to his or her heart's content. But Number 231's TV got better color than Number 175's, Number 19's was way too loud, etc. EatThis and UpYours, two of the kindest and most amenable Fartians to ever wait on a crowd, were recently roughed up over an improperly heated croissant, so now, with two staff in Recovery, YoMama was responsible for Monday's first shift all on his lonesome.

Patience is not just a Fartian virtue; it's a way of life and manner of thinking, as deep and irrevocable as the urge to assist and comfort. Earth had to be appropriated. *Had* to. After making their own solar system an atomic junkyard, terrans had set about turning the rest of the quadrant into a radioactive wilderness. The first emissaries from Fartia, coming in peace to beg for reason, were blown to smithereens by a quickly assembled International Guard, forcing the Fartians to subdue the planet by nullifying long-range weapons via microwave transmissions. They *had* to. It was that or write off the quadrant. After accepting effusive apologies, the United States president gave the conquerors the keys to the planet, free season tickets to Annie, and a signed CD of Bruce Springteen's Born In The USA. It was YoMama's practice to play a loop full blast whenever jingoism transported the clients.

"Number One," he said pleasantly. "Serving Number One."

Number One was a scrawny old woman with hair dyed the color of mercurochrome. YoMama recognized her from last week; he still suffered auralaches and an occasional nasalbleed. Number One immediately jumped on a table, lifted her skirt, and began thrusting her pelvis in YoMama's direction while clacking her false teeth and wiggling her tongue. The grievance made no sense to YoMama, but the roaring clients, banging their foreheads on chairs and tables, were clearly pleased by the gesture. YoMama, nodding and smiling, reached down to switch on the CD.

"*Bohn* in da USA," the Boss sang, right on cue and over and over and over and over. "*Bohn* in da USA! *Bohn* in da USA!" The crowd went wild. A youth with purple and green spiked hair smashed his face into the unbreakable glass separating YoMama from an imminent, much-supported, and long overdue Earth-whooping.

"You got that?" the youth screamed. He raised a victorious middle finger. "Number one, farthead, number one!"

"Serving," said YoMama.

The woman pulled her dress completely over her head, did a rapid stuttering flamenco on the tabletop, and spun onto the floor.

"Number Two," YoMama called. "Serving Number Two."

There was a terrible biting scuffle to his right. YoMama raised a flipper and hesitated. He prudently switched off the CD player. A raggedy man stepped free of the raggedy tussle and made his raggedy way to the window. "That's me, man. What I got to do around here to get some bus tokens? How'm I suppose to find a job walking all over the city? You wanna see the blisters on my feet, man?" He hauled a half-shod horror onto the narrow shelf beneath the glass.

YoMama pouted compassionately. "An abundance of jobs are to be found right here at the center, Number Two. Merely fill out this form and you will instantly be eligible for the occupation of your choice."

Number Two let his foot slide off the shelf. "I knew it, man, I just knew it. You had to get personal, didn't you? What you gotta know all about me for?"

"Merely for records, sir, and for the processing of payments. Your government insists that all accounts be scrupulously itemized."

"Who are you, man, the flipping F.B.I.? Jesus. A guy comes in asking for a little help, and you give him the third degree. And what's all that got to do with tokens, anyway?"

YoMama pulled out a roll of fifty. "Here are your coins, sir."

The man licked his lips. His eyes rolled back up. "What'm I gonna do with tokens, man? My car's sitting outside, and it's dry as a bone. You're telling me you want me to put a bunch of damn tokens in my gas tank? Ah, for the love of—"

YoMama placed the roll back in the drawer and pulled out a twenty. He slid it through the small opening at the bottom of the glass. Number Two snapped it up and raised it triumphantly. He was mobbed before he made the door.

"Number Three. Serving Number Three."

Number Three rose with the deadly certainty of a cornered cobra. Not since Betelgeuse had YoMama witnessed eyes so fixed and intense. Three wore an ankle-length mop of a trench coat over God knows what, and his hair and beard were so long and tangled it was difficult to tell where one began and the other gave up. Three's eyes held YoMama's all the way, his right hand repeatedly hurling down something unseen. When he reached the window he looked the little Fartian up and down before heaving a breath that fogged the glass lichen green:

"*He-e-e*-e-e shall riseth for your sins."

YoMama nodded energetically. This would be one of the messenger terrans, come to retell the fable of the man who flew up into a cloud. The Fartian pulled out a twenty and slipped it into the stainless steel tray.

Number Three, gravely insulted, snatched up the bill and stuffed it in a pocket. "Render unto Caesar..." he muttered viciously.

"Yes, yes," YoMama breathed, "that which is Caesar's!" He placed his chin on his folded flippers and looked on dreamily.

Number Three seemed to swell in his rags. "Let His Word come unto thee, that the inequities of the righteous brothers shall not be laundered in vain!"

YoMama sighed, gazing up at Number Three like a schoolgirl admiring a bubblegum dreamboat. The messengers were some of his favorites. They had the uncanny ability to orate for hours on end, reaching dramatic peaks and building again, never tiring, never varying. But after thirty-five minutes YoMama realized his hour was almost up; YouPrickYou would be coming on shortly, and YoMama was one-shy of his four-terran first shift quota. He hated to do it, but it was unquestionably cut-off time.

"That was absolutely lovely," he said. "Thank you so very, very much. The universe is actually a boundless entropic abstraction containing only polarized impulses in equipoise. The resultant impermeable electromagnetic spheres aggregate to a density appreciated by the senses as matter." He blinked affectionately.

Number Three's piehole worked round and round, seeking a center. His eyes gradually clouded, and his hand again hurled down the unseen; first with uncertainty, then with vicious comprehension.

"Number Four," YoMama called. "Serving Number

Four." From the corner of his eye he saw an identical Fartian through an adjoining door's glass. YouPrickYou smiled encouragingly. YoMama returned the gesture.

Number Four was a giant of a terran, with an arid and inflexible expression carved by years of loitering in the victimhood. He came, bless him, right to the point.

"How many hoop you spect me t'jump troo t'claim mah benefis? Ah wantsa know why Ah don't get no specs round here, an don't you be gibin me no innastella jive bout fillin out no goddam foams neither, cause Ah'll kick yo little greenman butt alla way back to da little greenman projects, an Ah ain's gonna need no Blew Crue to do, too, so *you*, foo, kin jus be *gibin* me mah benefis, right *now*, cause Ah ain's gots *time* to be playin yo spacemans games. Now you jus *opens* dat funny-money drawer, *sticks* in yo little retard flaps, and *Gib—Me—Mah—BENEFIS!*"

YoMama, smiling graciously, killed the speaker. One hand fell on the CD player, the other on his cubicle's mental survival kit: a microdot copy of the Fartian Ethical Code, a Sav-on photograph of a mindlessly cheerful Earth family, and a glowing lozenge-shaped vial containing the only dose of Infinity a self-respecting Grievance counselor would ever need. They say the sentience continuum's severance is instantaneous and painless. The original producers even claimed a kind of fuzzy ecstatic release. YoMama tapped twice on the kit's lid, the corners of his perpetually-cherubic mouth rising. He genially flipped the OPEN sign to its sweet dorsal side and hit the PLAY button. The Boss laid it down:

"*Bohn* in da USA! *Bohn* in da USA!"

YoMama beamed patiently at the contorted faces and deflected spit, his head gently rocking side to side, his whole damnable countenance an infuriating beacon. There was a soft tapping on glass. YouPrickYou was smiling charmingly while pointing from his left flipper to the wall clock and back. YoMama rose and eased open the door. The two embraced with extrastellar tenderness while the crowd blew kisses and showed limp wrists. YouPrickYou took the vacated seat, switched on the speaker, and turned the sign back to OPEN. One flipper killed the CD player while the other caressed the survival kit. A terran hurled a folding steel chair directly against the unbreakable window.

YouPrickYou smiled raptly through the glass. It was, after all, only Monday.

Elaine

There were worms in her mug.

Tiny white maggoty swimmers that peeked through the steam before diving back in her brew. Elaine blew them away and sipped without savor, more out of habit than desire. Her morose brown eye, rippling on the coffee's face, stared back, steamed over, dissolved.

A trained observer would note Elaine performed this ritual, as a regular break from her street-watching, approximately once every ninety seconds. To an untrained observer, she would appear intent and impatient, perhaps waiting on a tardy acquaintance.

That untrained observer now looked down at his own eggs and coffee, feeling Elaine lift her eyes.

It was one of those quirky events falling awkwardly into the norm; a square moment in a round day, a sentimental misstep in a routine dance of nods and evasions.

The elderly man looked back up. Their eyes met and held. It wasn't kismet; he found nothing attractive in the frumpish and pasty, rotund little woman with the bland ex-

7

pression. And Elaine, for her part, was not drawn to the spindly gray gentleman.

They both smiled.

Sun didn't break through clouds, or anything like that. It was a snapshot, dingy with caffeine, phlegm, and emotional disuse.

They looked back down.

Elaine caught herself peeking. The elderly man's eyes worked their way back up.

They smiled again, this time out of good old-fashioned nervousness.

Now it was more than uncomfortable. Though in adjacent booths, the two were only six feet apart, and situated dead-on: Crazy Dinah's All-Day Diner featured notoriously narrow tabletops, forcing facing customers to sit diagonally with their personal plates and silver.

The old man's voice was like cellophane. "Forgive me." His fluttering hands were lame pigeons, desperately side-stepping his mug, silver, and plate. "I didn't mean to make you nervous."

"That's okay," Elaine mumbled.

The gentleman coughed delicately. "Well, I guess I'm what you'd call a people person." His eyes searched the sidewalk. "I couldn't help noticing how you enjoy staring out this big old window." He smiled crookedly. "I guess that makes us both people people."

Elaine studied her coffee mug. "People—" she felt herself blushing, "people are…good."

The man, still smiling awkwardly, stuck his hand across the table. Long as his arms were, it was a gap too deep. He swung around to his table's facing bench, leaned over the back and tried again. "I'm Joe. Or Joseph, actually. Joseph Carten."

Elaine blushed until it burned. "Elaine Bushnelkopf." She shook hands timidly, immediately stuffing the unpracticed paw back in her lap.

He cocked an eyebrow. "Unusual last name, Lainey."

"From…from the Pennsylvania Bushnelkopfs. The family was in fertilizers."

"Can never get enough fertilizer. Umm…the Cartens, far as I know, were never into anything." He shrugged. "My dad was a serviceman. Air Force. He went down in Iwo."

"Oh!" Elaine blurted. "I'm just *so* sorry."

"Don't be. I never actually met the guy. No bridges built, no bridges burned."

"Then your mom must have been, well, very strong. Very dedicated."

He smiled engagingly. "That's what they say on the boulevard." That crooked old grin collapsed at her look of confusion. "I'm just kidding, Elaine. Just being, well, you know, sarcastic about the whole family thing."

"People shouldn't talk about their parents that way," Elaine muttered. She looked up quickly. "Not *you*, Joseph. I don't mean to be critical."

"Joe," he said, drumming his palms on the seat's greasy upholstery. "Look, I'm sorry, Elaine. You must have had super parents. Anyway, you're probably right. I should know enough to keep my big mouth shut." His eyes lit fractionally. "I've got to run, Lainey. It's been great jawing with you. Maybe we'll slam into each other again."

"I'd…" Elaine managed, "I'd like that."

"Ciao." Joe grinned and creaked to his feet. He dropped a five on his tab, smiled back at her, and whistled on out the door.

The worms resurfaced.

"So you scared off another one?"

Elaine didn't have to look up. Cassie was one of those unfriendly friends, functioning as both conscience and bully at the worst of times. Not that the worst of times were all that much worse than the best of times, and not that knowing someone execrable was a hell of a lot worse than knowing no one at all.

"He was in a hurry," Elaine breezed. "An important man."

Cassie laughed as she swept up Joseph's untouched plates, scraping his five off the table as though daubing a smear. "In a hurry? The only thing that'd make that old guy jump is a defibrulator." Her eyes gleamed. "But I do believe he got it up

9

for you, honey." She ticked a forefinger side to side. "Don't tell anybody, but I think little Lainey's got a fella."

"Stop it."

"Seriously, sweetheart. While you were staring out the window ol' Cassie was on the watch, as always. I think Mr. Hurry's got googly eyes."

"He was just being nice."

"Don't be so full of yourself. A girl has to take what she can in this world. And I like 'nice'." Facing Elaine, Cassie leaned halfway across the table, using her upper arms to meaningfully squeeze forth her very ample breasts. "If you think you can do better than these, sugar, then you just don't know men."

Elaine's eyes burned into her brew. The worms circled concentrically in response, making for the rim. Elaine blew so hard her coffee sprayed the tabletop. "Joseph's not like that. He's a gentleman."

Cassie cupped Elaine's free hand in hers. "Give me a break, Lainey. All men, God bless 'em, are 'like that'."

"No," Elaine whispered into her cup. "Not Joseph. Not Joe."

Elaine brooded all the way home. How could she have been so stupid. Joseph was the first man she'd spoken to, on anything remotely resembling an intimate level in…in…how *could* she have offended him like that. "Googly eyes." Absurd or not, the idea grew on her as she waddled across the courtyard to her tiny apartment. Like most of the building's disability recipients, Elaine's inability to pursue meaningful employment came from hormonally-triggered chronic despondency. But, unlike the rest of the girls, she was unable to find comfort in medication or company. Elaine was a drifting, stale dreamer, unwilling to focus on anything real.

She prepared her usual bath; lukewarm and not too full, tepid like everything else in her life. But for once she was prey to a forgotten impulse: Elaine exhumed her makeup kit and got liberal with the lipstick and liner. She added a capful of rose to the bath.

Elaine

The water took her as always, yet with an extra caress. Elaine soaped herself slowly with her left hand while her right slid over a breast and down her tummy. Two fingers made way for the third. But it wasn't wrong this time; it couldn't have been more right—that was Joseph down there, that was Joe. And Elaine's depression was lifting like fog.

That was Joey.

She wasn't exactly waiting for him, not in the literal sense. He'd never show, not after she'd embarrassed them both. But Elaine was on her fourth cup, and the sidewalk had lost all its appeal. She'd dolled herself up considerably. An ex-beautician neighbor took care of the hair and manicure, another loaned her a somewhat flattering dress. Elaine's mood shift was all over the building; in a heartbeat the secret was out, and her gentleman admirer the subject of endless gossip and guesswork. Elaine stank of Tabu from five feet away. In her purse was a neatly folded love poem, sealed with a kiss; part heartfelt rain and daybreak, part saccharine Hallmark cliché. Never had she been so nervous; it took the whole building to talk her into this. Elaine wanted to die. Or to live. It didn't matter. If he laughed, if he turned away, if he gave her one funny look—it didn't matter; she'd die. This was it, and she knew it. Her one and only chance for a man. For happiness, for comfort, for company. For all those things life had denied her, and granted everybody else in spades.

She carefully wiped the lipstick off her mug's porcelain rim. And again. Elaine sobbed and caught herself. She must look a mess. She'd gnawed away half her nail polish, the dress was bunching in all the wrong places, and tears and mascara don't mix. She couldn't breathe. And now she was hyperventilating. Hard to swallow. She took a sip and sobbed again.

The door chimes rang cheerfully, followed by Cassie's girlish squeal. Elaine couldn't believe her ears.

"Joey!"

At the same moment a dark brown step van pulled to the curb. The van's deep color provided a temporary backing for the window's pane, so that Elaine was able to monitor the

11

goings-on behind her by their reflection. The floral delivery van's huge heart-shaped logo formed a frame for the action at the register. Around this logo was set the legend: *Life Is For Lovers.*

Cassie was all over Joseph; kissing and petting and stroking and groping. In his gangly fingers dangled a large box of chocolates with a big pink bow.

Elaine turned, against her will. Cassie had Joseph's face in her chest now, but she swiveled long enough to squeeze her breasts with her arms while giving Elaine a triumphant wink and smile.

Elaine stumbled all the way home. Pedestrians stared curiously as she staggered off curbs, neighbors blanched and retreated into the shadows of their knowing lives.

She carefully plucked the flat packets off her medicine cabinet's bottom shelf, neatly laid out her makeup items round the tub's rim while the basin slowly filled.

Her hands trembled upon submerging. Elaine whimpered against the pain to come.

"*Shhh*," the razors whispered, "*shhh...shhh.*"

It didn't hurt the way she expected. The bath quickly went pink, only gradually turning red. Elaine raised her streaming arms, folded her fouled wrists across her chest. And Joseph appeared as a brooding transparency, waxing almost-real in perfect sync with the room's slow fade. She could see his mouth struggling to reach hers, could read his slow-motion lips, contorted by guilt and shame:

"I'm...Just...So...So...*Sorry...*"

"I," Elaine heard her voice reply, "forgive." But the sound was hollow, and leaning whence it came. And the air congealed, and the room dimmed, and Elaine's lips were utterly without sensation as Joey bent at the waist, passed out of passion's way, and kissed her once goodnight.

The Other Foot

"Kin Ah hep you?" said the big security guard at the door. The voice was an indifferent drawl. Gus looked at the man's nametag: CHAHLES.

"Yes, Chahles, I believe you may." Gus proffered his paperwork. "I've an appointment with a Mr. Earl Maven at nine sharp." He showed his pearly whites. "I came 'Earl'-y."

Chahles gestured over his shoulder at the packed waiting room. "So'd dey." A hundred and forty-one eyes glared at Gus eclipsing the opened glass door.

"Well!" Gus didn't lose the smile. "Where do I sign in, then?"

"Yo kin sign yo funny butt in on a empty chair; tha's if yo kin finds one."

Gus was intensely aware of his whiteness as he apologized his way to a steel folding chair with a collapsed back. He squinched in between a sleeping man and the biggest, meanest-looking woman he'd ever seen. He hadn't brought a book or newspaper, and wasn't particularly compelled to seek conversation. He should have known he'd be out of his element when the welfare processing office referred him to the outlet on Oprah and King, but he was new to the system, and not about to make trouble. Be quiet and polite. You'll always squeak through. Little by little this quiet, polite man found himself scrunching in while the surrounding tide just as gradually spread, until he resembled nothing so much as a squashed ivory exclamation mark in a smudgy text scrawl. Using his two available fingers, Gus pinched his paperwork into a tiny reading shield for his eyes. By eleven o'clock he'd read it over so many times it was a mantra to delirium. When at last he heard his name called he was barely able to slip from under the sleeping man's slobbering face and the big lady's glaring eye.

The clerk peered through the bulletproof glass with an expression skewed by a million threats and pleas. "You Gus Tremblen?"

"Yes, that's me."

"Say here your appointment for nine."

"Yes, that's right."

One eye rolled to the wall clock. "It eleven now."

"I realize that, sir. I was just called. I've been waiting patiently; very patiently."

"You sign in? I don't see your name on the sign-in."

"I wasn't aware…sir…I was told to take a chair, and complied. I had no idea that—"

"Who told you take a chair?"

"Well, it was the security guard. I believe his name is Chahles."

"Chahles told you take a chair?"

"He instructed me to…yes."

"You take orders from a security guard?"

"He didn't actually *order* me."

The clerk threw down his pen. "If that don't beat all." He flicked on the intercom. "CHAHLES, YOU COME TO WINDOW EIGHT."

A massive reflection grew on the glass like an overblown balloon.

"Chahles, you tell this man he not supposed to sign in on the sign-in?"

"Ah did not tell him nothin of the sort, suh."

"You tell this man he supposed to take a chair without signing in on the sign-in?"

"We didn talk about no sign-in, suh. Ah showed him where to sit, tha's all."

"He say he didn't want to sign in on no sign-in?"

"We didn talk about no sign-in, suh. Ah showed him where to take a chair."

The clerk shut Gus's file. "If that don't beat all."

A thin man in a suit slid through an adjacent door. "What's all this hollering?"

"This man don't want to sign in on no sign-in."

"Actually," Gus tried, "I'd be pleased to sign in, sir. There's some kind of misunderstanding, that's all."

The thin man adjusted his severe spectacles for an iron stare. He was one of the angriest looking people Gus had ever encountered. "Why didn't you sign in in the first place?"

"I wasn't aware—"

The thin man slapped down a palm. "If that don't beat all." He flipped open the daybook. "You see all these signatures on the sign-in? How come they gotta sign in on the sign-in and you don't gotta sign in on the sign-in? We just supposed to know you're here and dispense with procedure?"

"I..."

"Chahles, you tell this man he don't gotta sign in on no sign-in?"

"We didn talk about no sign-in, suh."

The suited man's eyes burned through the glass. "You refuse to sign in on the sign-in?"

"Sir, I—"

"Chahles!"

The balloon squeezed between Gus and the glass. Chahles's expression was dead-serious. Gus wasn't even aware of the next half-minute, so profoundly confused were his impressions. All he knew was he was standing in the doorway with his back to the street, and Chahles was looming like God Almighty.

"Now yo kin jus take yo crackajack bee-hind somewheres else."

"Lord!" swore the thin man, glaring through the glass.

He looked daggers at the clerk. "Next time someone don't wanna sign in on no sign-in, he trying to tell you he don't wanna be served. Why you bothering me with all this?"

"Chahles said—"

"You take orders from a security guard? If that don't beat all." He slipped back into his office. The Post-its were falling like leaves, the phone already ringing. He composed himself before lifting the receiver.

"Earlsy?"

"Bunny, I told you not to call me before lunch."

"But I miss you, sweetheart."

"I miss you too, sugar. We've talked about this a hundred times. Whenever I get a call on an outside line it's tallied, remember? I have to balance those calls against the client log."

"But my slipper," Bunny pouted.

"What about your slipper?"

"It got fried. In the microwave, somehow. You know the mink slippers; the pretty pink ones with the cute little diamonds that spell out I Worship You Bunny? Well, the right one got cooked, and it's all...*icky*. Now I have a slipper that says I Worship You, and a bare foot that don't say nothin. How'm I suppose to know *who* you worship, Earlsy?"

"But how did it get into the micro—"

"Don't yell at me!" Bunny wailed. "I'll get a restraining order, Earl Maven; you know I will. If I have to hop down to the station with one naked foot, I swear I'll protect myself."

"Bunny." Maven wiped a hand down his face. "Baby." He called up his online banking account on the office computer; another no-no. "Sweetheart." He typed in his password and went to accounts. His face fell further. "Darlin'!"

"Earlsy?"

"We're having kind of a tight calendar month, sugar. Must've been that rabbit-shaped hot tub."

"You said you loved my bunny bath."

"I do, Princess. It's just that—"

"DON'T YELL AT ME!" And Bunny was in serious tears.

"I promise you, Priceless. I *promise* you. Brand new slippers when I get home. Prettier than the last. As pretty as you."

"You'd better not be jerking me around, Earl Maven. The front door is locked if you come home empty-handed. Smooches?"

"Smooches," Maven said. "And when you're all dolled-up good as new we can play Counselor. I'll bring the Baileys. But please, Goddess, in the future try to remember that little rule about calls to the office. For right now I'll just write this off as a wrong num—got to go now, baby; another call." Maven punched the glowing button. His voice was instantly professional. "Earl Maven. Department of Welfare Adjustments."

"You're processing a claimant, one Gustave Merriwether Tremblen?"

Maven drummed his fingers on the desk. "Who's this?"

"My name is Harvey Gerbilstein, Mr. Maven, and I'm employed by the State of California to handle complaints from welfare applicants who feel they've been denied fair access to resources. We're in the building right next door. You know the one."

"No one has been denied anything to anything, Mr. Gerbilstein. Mr. Tremblen refused to sign the day's docket according to specified procedure, that's all. We are, by order, disallowed the processing of unruly claimants."

"Mr. Tremblen claims the security guard ejected him in a most threatening manner, and used the term 'cracker' in so doing. Now, Mr. Maven, a major part of my duties involves claims of behavior which may be construed as racist under article 749 of the State Discriminatory Code. I don't think we have to split hairs here."

Maven peeled off his glasses and pinched the bridge of his nose. "Security is not employed by the State of California. Any complaints will have o be directed to the proper offices." He slammed through his rolodex. "And I have the number right here."

"Wrong, Mr. Maven. Your department and ours have danced this dance before. Sukky Security is certified by the State, leaving California liable for any monetary damages incurred by successful complaints."

Maven dropped back his head. When he let it fall

forward it was wagging with frustration. "I can't help you, Gerbilstein. You'll have to take this up with my boss."

"Way ahead of you, Maven. Mr. Killwater was notified on his car phone prior to this call. I'd like you to know our little conversation, though brief, was extremely interesting. *So* interesting, as a matter of fact, that he decided to cancel his beloved golf match and proceed instead to your office for what I can only describe as a very-quickie conference. I'm not sure you're aware of it, Maven, but racism lawsuits regularly settle in the six figures. A man in Mr. Tremblen's shattered condition can expect lifetime compensation. Now, I've never been all that hot at tabulating mileage against traffic, but, if my calculations are anywhere near correct, Mr. Killwater should be showing up right…about…*now*."

A harumph and short bellow was followed by a tapering monologue from Chahles. Killwater, looking like he'd just swallowed a mouthful of glass, burst into Maven's office and slammed the door. The man was in his sixties, and at least as big as Chahles, but there was a bulldog-gruffness to his demeanor that made him appear larger than life.

"Maven! I've just been on the phone with a Harvey—"

"Gerbilstein," Maven sighed dismally, holding up the receiver. "He's right here."

Killwater snatched it as though reclaiming stolen property. "Gerbilstein? We're on conference!"

A ping and shift in the ether. "Done," came Gerbilstein's voice from the speaker.

"Is that complainant still there?"

Tremblen's voice, hard to pick up: "Um…" A scrape and throat-clearing. "*Yes*," the voice came back, clearer now. "I'm here."

"You were involved in an altercation with a member of our security staff?"

"Actually, it was more of a misunder—"

"Chahles!" The echo scraped paint off the lobby's walls.

A timid rapping.

"Open the damn door, Chahles!"

A quirky fluorescent corona displaced the unwelcome door.

"Did you threaten a Mister...a Mister..." Killwater snapped his fingers.

"Tremblen," came both Gerbilstein's and Tremblen's voices. Gerbilstein appended: "One Gustave Merri—"

"Did you threaten anybody, Chahles?"

"No suh. He don' wanna sign in on no sign-in, suh. Ah showed him where to take a chair, suh. Tha's all, suh."

"Why wouldn't he sign in on the sign-in?"

"He say he don' wanna sign in on no sign-in, suh."

Killwater's steamshovel jaw dropped. Speaking as much to himself as to the room, he muttered, "If that don't beat all."

Gerbilstein's voice was the snap of a whip. "Enough! Paperwork is already being processed in Tremblen vs. the State of California. Article 749.A.154,894,000-2B[12] states, unequivocally, that no applicant may be denied resources due to conditions of race, religion, gender, national origin, disability, height, weight, self-image, lack of character, hometown allegiance, or body aroma. Calling Mr. Tremblen a 'cracker' most definitely falls under the category of racial discrimination, and, since Sukky Security is on record as approved via the office of one Carlton Killwater, Mr. Killwater, along with his subordinate Earl Maven, are hereby notified of their status as defendants in Tremblen vs. California."

In the deafening silence came a sound like a squeal and clapping from Gerbilstein's end, then a very sober closure: "I'm afraid you'll have to cancel your golf date, Mr. Killwater. I'll be in touch. *Believe* me, I'll be in touch." The speaker went dead.

Killwater looked stunned. "Chahles?"

"Suh?"

"What went down between you and Mr. Tremblen?"

"He didn wanna sign in on no sign-in, suh. Ah showed him where to take a chair, suh. Tha's all, suh."

"Chahles."

"Suh?"

"Get the hell out of here."

The corona collapsed and the door whispered shut.

"Maven?"

"Sir?"

"Clear out your desk."

"Mr. Killwater, this is all a misunder—"

"*Maven?*"

"Sir?"

"Get the hell out of here!" Killwater drew open the door and shuffled out like the walking dead, his putter arm swinging listlessly.

The phone rang.

"Earlsy?"

"Bunny," Maven managed.

"Earlsy, my pearl necklace, you know, the one you brought all the way from Budapest, with the dark and light pearls next to each other that go one little bunny, two little bunny, one little...well, it got caught in the blender somehow, and now I don't have no one little bunny two."

Maven was drifting. "In the...blend—"

"DON'T SCREAM AT ME!"

Maven dropped the phone. In a trance, he pushed the personal contents of his office into a cardboard box labeled Trash Only, and dragged the box to his Mercedes. He somehow stuffed it all into the trunk and drove home like an automaton. The driveway was blocked by a pile of shirts and papers and very private miscellany. His photo albums, a collection of floppy-and compact disks, that prized foul ball off the bat of Itchy Krotchenscracher. Two patrol cars controlled the street on either side of Maven's drive. He left the Mercedes idling between cars and staggered to the curb.

An officer blocked his progress. "Are you Earl Maven?"

"Yes...I...I've..."

"Mr. Earl Maven, the Los Angeles Police Department is responding to a call of sexual harassment by one Bunny B. Goldigeur, a professed resident of these premises. It is my duty to inform you, sir, that if you are approaching said premises with malice intended, you will be placed under arrest for the sake of said party. That's all. Nothing personal. If you are indeed owner or lessor of said premises you are hereby awarded license to claim any and all properties deposited upon this drive. For the sake of Ms. Goldigeur, however, you may not breach said premises."

"My...property...gather my..."

"But no farther." There was a rumble and whirrrrrrrrrrr behind them. Maven was too dazed to turn. "You may now claim said personal belongings from said drive. Said one last time: if you approach Ms. Goldigeur or said lodgings you will be placed under arrest. Enough said. Do we understand each other?" The whirrrrrrrrrrr became an elongated grind.

"Yes, sir...I—please forgive me if I have in any way—"

"Five minutes," the officer articulated. "You have five minutes to appropriate your property. Not because it's property-specific. But because you've been warned."

"I—"

"Four minutes, Mr. Maven. Move it."

The whirrrrrrrrrrr became a tearing, grinding scream! Maven turned. His Mercedes was being dragged up the spine of a Grabby's Tow truck!

The officer shook his head balefully. "No parking in the street. You know that, Mr. Maven. I am, due to your circumstances, waiving the curb infraction. You may reclaim your vehicle from Venal's Tow." He patted Maven's shoulder. "Have a nice day."

The other car's door swung open and a female officer emerged. Pretty little thing. She charged up like a bouncer on a bad night.

"Are we having trouble here, Officer Wyatt?"

"He has three minutes," said Wyatt.

She turned on Maven, her expression fierce. "*What is your problem*, sir?"

"Two."

"I...she...misunder—"

"One minute."

Bunny wailed from an upstairs window.

The female officer got right in Maven's face. "Sir, I need you to place your hands behind your back."

"Let's go," Wyatt said. "It's domestic. He's locked out."

The officers returned to their respective vehicles. Wyatt leaned over his car's roof. "Your minute's up, Mr. Maven. Get an attorney." The head disappeared. The cars drove off. Bunny slammed the upstairs window.

Maven knelt to his pile like a sinner at an altar. His eyes fell on a shopping cart with a broken wheel, resting half on the curb. Maven used this cart to hold his belongings. He looked around for a place to store it. The garage would only open from without by way of the Mercedes' dash sounder. There was a tool shed out back, and Maven had the key, although technically using the yard might be construed as entering the premises. As though reading his mind, that female officer nosed her patrol car around the corner.

Maven grimly jerked his cart along the sidewalk, not daring to look back. First thing was to get the Mercedes back. There was room in the trunk, with a little creative stuffing, for both the cart's and the office's articles. He'd find a decent hotel. Hell, he'd sleep in the damn car if he had to—Maven's will was returning with each forced jerk of that dragging front wheel. The car continued to pace him, slowly loitering a hundred yards back. It grew on Maven: he was going to be cited for shopping cart theft; he could feel it. Just to screw him deeper. The female officer probably sided with Bunny, probably profiled Maven solely from the context of a thousand spousal abuse calls. He hunched his shoulders and gritted his teeth as he lurched along, his glasses hanging at an angle. Maven wobbled around the corner and down the short block leading to the pedestrian tunnel adjoining Parasite Park. He was forcing the officer's hand: she'd have to stop him now if she meant business. The car halted in the intersection and sat idling as he shook his way into the unlit, graffiti-riddled tunnel. The car moved on and Maven heaved a sigh of relief.

"What you doing with my cart, man?"

Maven squinted at the blur. He adjusted his glasses. There was more than one blur; several, actually, and they were moving to block a retreat.

"Yours?" Maven wondered. "My apologies. A misunder—"

"Tell you what, homey;" said the first blur, now shaping up as a rather large individual with a shaved and tattooed head, "I'm sick of the damned thing. So what I'm gonna do is sell it to you, see?"

Maven was thrown into a headlock from behind. His

arms were restrained, his wallet removed. The first individual straightened Maven's tie and fluffed his hair. "On second thought, I'm gonna let you keep it. Like I said, I'm sick of the thing."

Only the cart at his waist prevented Maven from dropping to his knees. "Take the cash! I don't care; just leave me my credit cards. They're no good to you!"

The tattooed man grinned. "Are you kidding?" He flashed the cards like a straight flush. "Better than cash!"

"My I.D.!" Maven wailed.

The man shook his head. "*My* I.D."

And they were gone, swallowed up in the dark tunnel before the el.

Maven stood there in shock for a good five minutes. When he surfaced he realized the worst thing he could do was lose track of his wallet. That lady cop might still be nearby, perhaps even now watching the tunnel from the park side, waiting for him to exit. If Maven could finger those thugs while the crime was still hot he'd be back in business. He pushed the cart shuffling, licking his lips eagerly.

Maven rounded the tunnel's el and daylight hit him like a fist. The park appeared deserted. As the window of visibility grew he found himself slowing, knowing the worst. He stepped out into a park abounding with litter, gang graffiti, and dog waste. But no people.

Make that one person. At Maven's feet was an old homeless man with one leg, a can of Steel 211, and an empty smile. "That's a *nice* cart, friend!"

And Maven was in tears. He dropped on his butt by the old man, accepted a drink. "Don't be so down," the homeless man crooned. "Things'll get better." He admired Maven's suit. "B'sides, you look like you do all right for yourself. What's your racket?"

"Welfare adjuster," Maven moaned. "Ex."

"Then what's to worry? You know the system."

Maven sat right up and stared at the old man. Gummy or not, that was the sweetest smile he'd ever seen.

At nine sharp Maven stood in the welfare office doorway at Duke and Falwell. He was unshaven and hadn't bathed.
He'd slept in his clothes and gone without breakfast. But he'd
never felt so alive.

"Can I help you, sir?" asked the guard, a ruddy, heavyset
man with a crewcut and thinning brown moustache. Maven
looked at his nametag—BUFORD—then at the rows of staring
white faces. He smiled toothily.

"Ah comes to sign in on da sign-in!"

"Sir?" The guard was obviously miffed; he could feel
the quiet faces watching intently. "Do you have an appointment,
sir?"

"Ah gots a 'pointment wit yo mama."

The light brown eyes turned umber. Buford said through
his teeth, "Sir, I'm afraid there's been some sort of misunder—"

"Well, if that don't beat all!"

"Get the hell out of here—"

"Oh, yeah?"

"—just keep your stupid ass on the street where it be-
longs—"

"Say *what?*"

"—and never darken our door again."

Maven rolled his eyes. "*Excuse* me? Did you say never
'darken' your door?"

"You heard me."

"Bufie, does the name Harvey Gerbilstein mean anything to you?"

"No, sir, it most certainly does not!"

Maven faced the street and bent at the waist, offering his
scruff and rear. "Then let's get this train a'rollin'."

Pluribus

"Ladies and gentlemen...*the Fartian Ambassador!*"

Spotlights searched wildly while the orchestra struggled through the Fartian anthem. It was a tough work, written as it was for a seventeen-piece ensemble of bowed genitalia and flatulating choir, but the theme had been transposed by the Pocoima Pops to an arrangement featuring synthesized piglets over symphonic kazoos. The strutting Ambassador appeared genuinely rapturous, while the terrans had difficulty humming along and feigning enjoyment. But the audience got positively silly as soon as the orchestra picked up that good old English drinking song, the American National Anthem. So ugly was the Fartian Anthem, in fact, that our own agonizing anthem seemed downright lovely by comparison.

The Ambassador slapped his flippers up the podium's concealed steps, cleared his gasbox, and pressed his rubbery lips right up against the microphone.

"Gerkils and plissyfogs. I deeply thank you for your attendance. As arranged by this forum's coordinators, the program will proceed as follows: a brief statement composed by our First Fartian, a regulated interrogation from the esteemed panel, and a question and answer session with the audience.

"Now to the First's Address, in flubschaum may he bifurcate.

"'Wonderful people of Earth. It has been our great fortune to serve you, and with boundless excitement we look forward to your continued ridicule and abuse. However, there remain wide dissimilarities in our cultures, and we therefore humbly and repeatedly beg forgiveness for any and all trouble we may have caused. Assimilating as your grateful slaves requires an adjustment to Earth customs we still find puzzling. Like your practice of treating restaurants, cinemas, sidewalks, and roadways as personal living rooms, bedrooms, and lavatories; this strikes us as most peculiar. We Fartians behave respectfully in public, and are literally incapable of giggling, guffawing, or bellowing in the faces of strangers. But we are working on it. Your diversity astonishes us; you come in so many colors and types. Speaking frankly, yet with the utmost admiration, we must inform the host nation that we do not understand how this "melting pot," as you call it, can contain so many persons, with so much good fortune, who nevertheless voice a common plaint of victimhood—but rest assured that our interstellar convoys are even now bringing vast cargos of wealth and luxuries beyond your imaginations. We can only hope it will be enough. Then there is your Earthling insistence on a cosmological creator, who made you, us, and everything else… honestly, people of Earth, we look and we look and we look, but…nothing. We simply can find no trace of this entity. There is almost too much to ponder. Such as the predisposition of your females to paint themselves like circus performers, run around near-naked in public, and titter in the manner of developmentally challenged children; this is most foreign to our way of thinking. Yet you will be quite pleased to learn that our Fartian plissyfogs, in an attempt to emulate their astounding terran counterparts, now proudly flaunt their danglepumps and viletrenches, and perform slop-and-pierce operations wherever and whenever possible. And thank you again and again, but we sincerely do not urgently require, as you so earnestly reiterate, insurance policies and monster wheels for our spacecraft, additional toner for our nonexistent printing equipment, in-vessel family tanning spas, or one-of-a-kind, won't-last-forever, get-it-while-it's-hot lakeside acreage smack in the middle of the Mojave Desert. Your terran consideration for our well-being never ceases to amaze us. And your leaders! Most regal they are, to be sure, and most gracious…yet, on our home planet, leaders are selected for their wisdom, compassion, and eagerness to serve. All over this gorgeous globe we encounter premiers, kings, and presidents, all chosen for their photogenic qualities and ability to intimidate. Most peculiar. Also, there is this ubiquitous and absolutely mystifying terran preoccupation with cell phones. The ability of humans—even adult males—to "make chitty-chat" ad nauseum, in restaurants, in automobiles, in hospitals and morgues, originally struck us as so rude and unbecoming even a Fartian slimeswiller would flumpergaggle with shame. Thankfully, our Department of Terran Analyses has reached its long-sought conclusion. By noting the striking similarities between social humans, dung beetles under duress, and Fartian spore squatters in heat, we have inferred a biochemical catalyst causing a kind of brainleak only remedied through electronic venting. So you will surely be pleased to learn we are responding to the eighteen billion-plus tally from your famous WishList Foundation; the identical wish from everybody from little Suzie Sunnymuffin of Clinton's Folly, Arkansas, to Muhammed-Mash Muhammed Muhammed Comma Muhammed Osama-Obama Muhammed Comma Ramalama Muhammed Slashan' dash-Muhammed Muhammed Muhammed of New Rubble, Iran. And *so-o-o-o*…(here the orchestra recreated a Fartian drum roll using perforated mahogany oars on vats of semi-congealed oatmeal)—*stereo cell phones for everybody'!"*

The crowd's roar made an instant celebrity of anybody green, rectally-gilled, and multi-flippered. Terrans, immediately dialing up audience members to either side, slapped their personal cell phones temple-to-temple in anticipation, launching endless urgent dialogues on everything from American Idol to Wheel Of Fortune to just whose turn *is* it to take out the garbage, anyway. Women glazed and ran on and on without breath or forethought, men squealed and stamped their clod-hoppers with delight. A great "chitty chant" began in the front rows, picked up quickly by the room: "Chitty-chat! *Chitty*-chat! *Chitty-chat!*"

The beaming Ambassador gave a downstroke with his flipper. The Fartian Anthem began and the crowd died on a dime. The orchestra shrieked and farted to a close.

"Thus ends our First's Address." The Ambassador, looking to the monitor with embarrassment, raised a flipper to his forehead before placing it politely on his chest. "It states here that, having reverently saluted this forum's host nation, I am to gratefully gush green over...Exxon, a distiller of liquid carcinogens...Avis, a noted hard-trier...and the McDonald's Corporation, proud purveyor of the exciting new Flavor-Free® McMulch Burger and sucrose-smothered McGooey Pie. In flub-schaum may they liquefy."

The Fartian turned to a trio of podia on his right. "I will now joyously accept questions from our sincere and erudite panel."

Moderator One's question was up and out before his colleagues were halfway through their "Mister Ambassador"'s.

"How long have we been promised this convoy, Ambassador? And why the big secret about its contents? You are obviously aware of our trepidation concerning the possibiliies of an insidious takeover."

The Ambassador raised a hand, though the audience was hushed. "Kindly allow me to entertain your queries in the order they were delivered. According to my terran chronometer, the duration of this promise is, as of this check, two minutes and thirty-two seconds. Secondly, there are no secrets regarding the convoy's cargo; as usual we are importing precious stones and metals, with an accent on diamonds, gold, and silver as per your demands, along with an abundance of the Fartian schlemburgers and fizzpops your people so urgently crave. And as to your charming notion concerning a 'takeover,' as you term it, our vessels, officers, and records are entirely at your disposal, as always." He smiled angelically.

The center moderator, a hard-boiled lady anchor from Earth Only News Network, raised her voice so stridently the first moderator was forced to back down. "*Mister* Ambassador! These are simple questions; there is no need to be evasive.

Furthermore, I have irrefutable data proving children at Obama Elementary were taken ill after gorging on these 'fizzpops' of yours. How do you answer this charge?"

The Ambassador's whole face pursed. "This is unbearable news! They will be all right? Certainly we will recall the fizzpops."

"I hardly consider tummy aches and missed classes 'all right,' Ambassador!"

There was a scuffle in the audience, and a man with a bullhorn called out, "*Indian giver!*" Immediately a nearby party of Native American businessmen began hacking at the troublemaker with pickets. Secret Service agents mauled their way to the spot. Pockets of unrest formed rapidly in the crowd.

"Please..." the Ambassador tried. "We are doing our very best."

Moderator Three thrust forth an accusing forefinger. "The market will not bear a glut of gold and silver! How long, Ambassador, before these precious metals are no longer so precious?"

"Forgive us," the Ambassador wept, "for our unconscionable insensitivity and egregious misinterpretation of your magnifi—"

"Ladies and gentlemen, the Fartian Ambassador has been shot! Ladies and gentlemen, the Fartian Ambassador has been shot! This is Dick Strickly on your morning driveby with the news, weather, sports, and a crib full of goodies. Apparently a heckler at the Schwarzenegger Convention Center splattered the Fartian Ambassador from here to Andromeda before being taken down by a drunken contingent of Secret Serv—*HONK HONK*—what's that? Appears we have a winner on Strictly Dick's Gangbanger Gazebo. It's Li'l Snoop from Compton, California. How they hangin', Snoopster? Get off your feet, grab a ho and a seat, 'cause you're the eighty-seven thousandth caller to correctly identify Hilary and Bill Clinton as a couple of complete—hold on a second, this just in. *Ladies and gentlemen, the Fartian Ambassador wears a shirt! Ladies and gentlemen, the Fartian Ambassador wears a shirt!* We go straight to our

live feed with Rusty Carbunkle at the Center. How they hangin', Ruster?

Dick, it's pandemonium here at the Schwarzenegger. Apparently an Art Bell devotee, claiming his gang-raped great grandmother was teleported into a Fartian wormhole, produced a handgun, shouted "Bring back the King Sisters!" and took out all mankind's frustration on that little girly worm from the big green apple. Panic swept the Center. Don King threw in the towel, Stephen King spun off a pointless Haunted Convention Center trilogy, guest speaker Rodney G. King broadsided the ambulance rushing Larry King and B.B. King to Martin Luther King Hospital, and the Gay Scouts Marching Band has been postponed indefinitely. The city is in flames. Right now Bono is furiously organizing the entire Western hemisphere for a Full Day Of Really Bad Music, Donald Trump is urging the Fartian Four Hundred to join him in a Sweet Deal Seminar, and, and…I can see Paris Hilton fighting off her admirer, Dick, and it looks like she's heading our way. Paris! Paris! How do you think this bodes for world peace? Can we get your thoughts on the obtuse ramifications of intergalactic telemetry when digitized according to Euclidian—Dick? Dick? The crowd is taking the stage! I see flags, Dick. Old Glory, the Blue-Green Globe, the Turkistani National. I think this is it, Dick. We're coming back! There's Gallagher and Oprah and the Hulkster and Stallone, fighting for the camera. There's Imus and Rush and Leykis and Stern, fighting for the microphone. This just in: Governor Schwarzenegger is riding his stationary bike down from Sacramento, and President Bush has declared complete victory for Fartia. Oh my God, Dick, here come the big guns! There's Siegfried and Roy with the ghost of Liberace. Sharpton and Sandler and Big Bird and Barbra. They're holding hands, Dick, it's working—no, wait; there's a roundhouse from Oprah to the chin of Rickenbacker. Orville's down, but he pops back up. Now it's all Pauly paling in the spotlight. A ruckus to his left and—*No!* Mike Tyson just bit off Pee Wee Herman's ill-used body part. They're carrying him off screaming. Oh my God, oh my God, oh my God! *It's Michael Jackson*, leading an entourage of little blond boys in fishnet! The crowd's going *insane!* Oprah and Sally, scrabbling to meet him. Carrot Top and Potato Head, struggling to be heard. There's Marcia and Johnny and Goofy and Waldo…the audience erupts—it's a mindless rush; a mad river of posers and wannabes. I can't see what's happening—the multi-talented Moonwalker is being mobbed. But there's Stern, towering obscenely. He shoves his way through, and now it's King meets King, Dick! Stern grabs The Glove and jealously guards his prize. What's he doing with it? He's pulling down his pants and—dear God, Dick! They're calling out Security! Now they're hosing him down with fire extinguishers! The show can't go on! But put away those remotes, people, 'cause here comes Gilbert and Bobcat and Tyra and Star. Ryan and Rosie and Rodney and Regis. The Verizon Geek, Mr. Rainbow Wig, Subway's Jared, and Shrek in drag. They're line-dancing, Dick, they're kicking up their heels—it's Earth's finest hour! Paparazzi swarming like flies on doggie don't! Cameras flashing! Spotlights spinning! Mother of Mercy, Dick—*Tyson's gone bananas!* He's snapping at Snoop Dogg, spitting on Spike, stomping on Stevie…*he's breaking his chains!* No more cameras! No more cameras! Somebody kill those lights! Somebody call the Air Force! Oh, the humanity. The stage is collapsing, the curtain's coming down. Wait! Wait! There's an enormous gasp from the crowd. The spotlights swerve, the cameras swing…*it's Elton John,* dressed in a stunning rainbow-patterned mink-and-nylon body stocking with rhinestone-studded peacock feathers, floor-length see-through diamond-dusted condom hat, platform-heeled pink suede elf boots, and swirling gold lamé bridal train. He waddles across what's left of the stage to Jackson's side. Their eyes meet and sparkle. Jackson drops his best boy, John's glasses fog over. They throw out their arms. They reach in and embrace…and now they're…they're…oh for the love of—who knew two people could actually do that…but these aren't just regular guys, Dick. No siree, Betsy. This is talent at its most entertaining. The crowd whoops and whinnies. They want an encore. But how do you follow a performance like that? Well, color me crimson and kiss my fat aunt Fannie—here come the Rockettes on walkers, the Spice Girls in straitjackets, the Blue Man Crew on unicycles, butting their heads and slapping their thighs. I'm more than proud, folks, I'm patriotic-proud. And it just makes you want to shake your head and ponder your—Dick! Dick! There's a fanfare from the pit! The giant TV screen's coming down! I can't believe it—it's live from the White House. The crowd falls hushed. The whole world holds its breath. There's the Oval Office, and the Stars and Stripes. The President's at his desk. He's looking around. He's staring at something on his hand. I'm not sure he knows he's on camera, Dick. Mr. Bush! Look straight ahead! No, over *here!* Mr. Bush...they're going to commercial, Dick. But that's okay; who could ever get enough Cal Worthington. And the crowd is definitely in favor of the moment. It's toy flags and cell phones, it's corn dogs all around. There's Latifah and Latoya, Osama and Cher, Milli and Vanilli with Mr. Bean in between. The crowd is just ecstatic. They're flicking their Bics in acknowledgement. What's that? A commotion in the back...*it's O.J. and Tyson*, Dick; they're going toe to toe! Kill those lighters! Ban those Bics! A roar and a scream—dear God in heaven—somebody call a veterinarian. It's on, it's on—the screen's on again! We're back live at the Oval Office, Dick! They've fixed the problem. There's the Stars and Stripes. There's the President at his desk. He's looking all around. Now he's staring down at the carpet. He seems to have dropped his cookie, Dick. The camera zooms in. The President raises his head and knocks himelf sillier. He stares at his hand. Now he's looking all around. They're going to commercial. But that's okay; who could ever get enough Larry Miller. Rosanne grabs her crotch and makes for the mic! The band breaks into To Hell With The Chief. It's toy flags and cell phones, it's Slurpees all around. What an inspiration—the whole crowd's standing at attention; they're making chitty-chat while saluting the screen! We're back, baby, we're back in control. Do you hear that great big cheer, you puny green invaders? Are you following this? Well, you'd better get ready for Round One, because, damn your nasty little hides, the Fartian War has begun!

The Other Side

The whole gang pressed in when Michael began foaming. His eyes rolled back, flickered a bit, and seemed to squeeze into his skull. A great breath filled his lungs. Sherri and Whiz grabbed the arms, Dale and Cindy the legs. Michael's back arched and his hands clenched. Two seconds later he was thrashing wildly. A long shudder worked up from his toes, tightened his sphincter, and snapped back his head. He lay absolutely still. No one said a word; all eyes were on that wracked face. Slowly a bloody spume formed at each corner of the boy's mouth. A red ooze broke from one nostril and rolled down a cheek, shiny in the amber haze of streetlamps. The gang looked up simultaneously. Their eyes all flashed, and their common sentiment was spontaneous:

"Cool!"

"So tell me what it was like," Sherri prodded. "I mean, tell me what it was really like."

Michael hemmed evasively. But he'd always been shy; a distant boy with a sweet interior. Sherri liked him that way. The other girls went for the jocks and the jerkoffs, but Sherri found it more fun cracking the shell than buffing the surface.

"It was like they say," Michael mumbled. "'You've never really lived'—"

Sherri completed Morté's most popular catch phrase, "—'until you've seen the other side.' So what was it like? The other side. Were you dead?"

Michael turned. "I couldn't have been, Sher. Or I wouldn't be here. Nobody comes back."

"I know, I know. But what was it *like*? Did you *feel* you were dead?" She giggled at her own notion. "Dead people don't feel."

"I felt…" In the car's half-light Michael's face was not unlike that rictus under the streetlamps. "I felt…things I wasn't supposed to feel. I saw things I wasn't supposed to see."

"Like *what*?"

"Like…things."

"Okay, Mikey." At that most unmanly nickname the blue hollows of his face turned purple. "Okay, *Michael*. I'll just have to find out for myself."

"No, Sherri. You can't do that. You mustn't!"

She gave him her patented peeved look. "Don't play control-freak with me, Michael. Everybody's doing Morté. 'What's good for the goose,' right? Why should guys get to have all the fun?"

"It's not fun! Not fun. Only…"

Sherri turned away. "Christ, Michael, you look like something out of George Romero. If it's no fun, the hell with it."

"Only…"

"Only?"

"I'm going back in."

"Michael."

He kept his eyes shut. There was no way to close his ears.

"Michael."

That was what he hated about life. How do you tell an adult, before he gives you all that crap about having so much to live for, that there's just so much to die for—

"Michael."

He opened his eyes. The stupid shrink was watching him as though he were a fish in an aquarium. Stupid pince-nez. Stupid little goatee. Stupid folded hands in a stupid brown suit.

"If these questions are making you uncomfortable, we can start with something fresh. But you should know your father is paying a lot of money for this session, and will only be that much harder to live with if he feels we didn't make progress."

"I realize that, sir."

"Now, Michael…peer pressure can cause youngsters to make decisions that are not in their best interest. This drug, with its ability to temporarily mimic the cessation of life, is achieving notorious popularity among the young." Dr. Vies closed his eyes and drew his sensitive fingers to his lips. He rocked his narrow head and those arched fingers metronomically, saying, "Tch, tch, tch." It was an effete move. A stupid move. "Interviewed participants invariably describe an episode of complete darkness, soon followed by a gradual, and most agreeable, return to full consciousness. They claim a profound and powerful sense of resurgence, of being born anew. They claim, too, that this interlude of mock demise is without sensation, and figureless. But you, Michael, according to your father, girlfriend, and two paramedics, claim to have experienced a sort of visitation, which you have difficulty depicting verbally." Vies's Mona Lisa smile fell flat. "Now, I have always found the argument for an afterlife, or an out-of-body experience, intensely provocative. I'm sure you have too; you are an intelligent young man. You need not feel pressured here; not in this private room, not with me. Understand that my profession's ethical code ensures complete confidentiality between doctor and patient, or, as I like to portray the relationship, mentor and friend. So please feel free to be just as forthcoming with me as with your young comrades. Our conversation, I assure you, will not leave this room." He leaned forward, causing Michael to just as levelly lean back. "So what did you experience, son? What did you see or feel? In your own words, please, and take your time."

Michael froze, weighing his options. He could stall, he could lie, he could tell someone what he'd been through. Someone who wouldn't laugh. He licked his lips and leaned forward.

"First I got real sick," he whispered. "Then I felt cold and numb; I couldn't move, sir, not at all."

Vies nodded. "The drug's effects impersonate rigor mortis, but with a semi-conscious twist."

Michael relaxed his shoulders. His voice approached normal volume, and Dr. Vies leaned back. "Everything stopped. I was dead, sir, not 'like dead.' It was over. I stopped being alive."

"Yet you perceived this. You were 'aware' of being dead. Do you not see the contradiction?"

"Of course. But I still died. I mean, the conscious thing you're talking about was the old me. I left that. Honestly, sir, I couldn't feel anything, couldn't see anything, couldn't smell or taste anything…what happened was different. But it was still happening."

Vies removed his pince-nez and fastidiously polished the lenses with a silk-embroidered kerchief while staring at his knees and nodding apologetically.

Worse than effete. A nancy-boy. A damned fruit was trying to get inside his head. It was obscene; more obscene than the stickiest locker room banter. Good old life, right back in the saddle. It became important to keep talking before that horrible anal-retentive cartoon resumed control of the conversation.

"There was someone else in there…over there…wherever. Someone who was talking to me—but he wasn't speaking. It was scary, but it didn't matter, because I wasn't there. I mean *it* wasn't there. Am I making any sense?"

Vies's nod was encouraging. Michael's narrative had achieved a monotonic caliber, a quasi-hypnotic state clearly suggestive of catharsis. At this point it's important an analyst become as motionless as possible, prod only in the affirmative, and fade to black. Teenagers like Michael—insular, diffident, sensitive—are excellent subjects when afforded retreat.

"I knew he—it—was speaking to me, because he called me by name—even though I didn't actually *hear* him. He didn't want me to come in. He said—he said when the body dies the consciousness goes on, but it's not like what everybody says it is."

Vies was careful. "You were encountering a 'soul,' then? An angel, perhaps, come to lead you to the afterworld?"

Michael jerked back to the real. "No! What did I just tell you, doctor? I said he didn't want me to come in. I said it was different. I'm not talking about some white light at the end of a tunnel."

Vies sat perfectly still. The room submerged imperceptibly, the air seemed to clot, the tension was gradually replaced by that same low hum of subtly intimate pause.

"Michael. I would like to perform a kind of experiment now. Do not be alarmed. I am going to diminish the amount of visible light in this room. The purpose of this procedure is to reduce distraction, thereby enabling your closer approximation of that state you so urgently wish to recover." The phrase *urgently wish* was a seed, planted with an almost sultry undertone.

"I'm...I...I don't want to be in the dark...not with another man."

"Do not be alarmed," Vies repeated. "I shall remain seated, and so shall you." He rose and turned a dimmer behind the bookcase, returned to his chair. "There. The atmosphere is much more amenable to free speaking." The room was bathed in a sedative drear. Michael could still see, but Vies was more like a ghost than an analyst. Now they were both dead men.

"He said," Michael went on, in that prior drone, "he said that being on the other side is an elecatro...eleckamagnets..."

"Electromagnetic?" Vies wondered, one nancy brow arched. "You are a student of physics, then, Michael?"

Michael appeared to wince in the dimness. "No. He said it was that electric magnet jive you just said. A phenomenon, if I got that right, that was the opposite of life—negative activity, he said. I don't know science junk, sir, I can only tell you what he told me. And that was that when the physical body dies, the electrical stuff that kept it going ends up in another place; a place where regular-life things don't apply. You have memories, you have feelings, but you don't have thoughts or goals or anything like that."

Vies's voice was soft and even. "This is most understandable, Michael. One would have little use for goals without a corporeal vessel. But you speak of feelings. They were warm? They were peaceful? What did your friend have to say about feelings?"

Michael's mouth fell open and his face took on a ghastly pall. "Not my…friend."

Vies wanted to kick himself. "This visitor; the apparition. What were its feelings, its impressions?"

"Worms," Michael intoned. "Worms and maggots, eating you…forever. Horror. Pain. Sickness. Screaming all around. But no sound. Worms. Always worms…" The youthful contours passing from his face were just as steadily replaced by planes and crags of an indigo hue. The eyes now goring Vies were arid and fixed. The analyst's nostrils twitched at a nauseating odor.

Vies tore at his collar. He coughed, rose, and stepped to the dimmer. Michael's body was stiff and scrunched in his chair, his face drawn, his eyes hollow.

"Michael." The boy didn't respond. "Michael!" Vies opened his office door and leaned out. "Miss Carter. I would like you to dial 911, please." He looked back into the room. Michael appeared to be surfacing; the blast of light was calling him back. "Hold that command, Miss Carter." Vies reached in and turned the room lights up to full. Michael blinked rapidly. A moment later he was looking all around; a nervous teen unhappy with his surroundings.

Vies stood thoughtfully in the doorway, caught between two worlds.

"Michael."

The boy looked up.

"Your session is over, Michael. I told your father you would call him at home when we were done. He is understandably anxious. I would like you to make that call now. Miss Carter, will you please buzz the door so Michael may phone home." He allowed a lot of elbow room for the boy's exit. "Do not be worried, son. Your father loves you very much, and agrees it is best you have plenty of space after this session. You are free to walk home rather than be picked up. He only wants to hear your voice, and to know you are feeling better. As do I."

There was a long electrical buzz. Michael hesitated, took a few steps. The buzz was reprised. Michael stepped into the receptionist's office. Miss Carter looked through the glass. At a nod from Vies she walked into the back room and made for a file cabinet. Vies gave Michael a little nancy smile before sliding into his office. Michael dialed the number and cupped the mouthpiece with his free hand.

"It's Michael. I know you are. But I can't talk now. Just be at Cindy's in ten minutes. I'll be on foot. Yes. Bring me a hit, man, and I don't want to get burned. Yes, yes, yes. I'm going back in. Yes."

The Book Of Ron

(Being a Highly Authorized clarification of events surrounding
the Creation and early development of man)

—By Way Of Introduction—

I am one of the few lucid individuals to have actually
seen and heard God—an honor He no longer bestows lightly.

He is not particularly ravenous for company—embarrassed as He is by the blunder of humanity—and now limits His
interviews to those possessing a certain stolidity of constitution.
The bungling-humans Headache has persisted for thousands of
years now (thanks a bunch, scribes, for a convoluted spiritual-
ity, an ever-splintering credo, and a mangled and incomprehen-
sible testament), so I was approached with caution.

Here was the Great and Wonderful God's dilemma: The
most important, meaningful, and profound document in the universe—the Word, the History of all that Is—was set down
millennia ago in a turgid, incredibly overdrawn, wholly unread-

able style. How in the world was He to win over an endless stream of increasingly sophisticated seekers while saddled with a work that guaranteed the rapid zoning-out of even the most avid reader?

What God needed was a contemporary writer—someone attuned to the easygoing, near-glutted appetites of modern Americans—but one with an attitude. What He needed was a cynic, a thinking man; someone not so susceptible to the emotional pitfalls of faith as to immediately revert to ecumenical gobbledygook; *you* know, all that outdated stuff that makes the Old Bible so hard to get into.

But man, was I a tough nut to crack.

In the first place, I've never bought into magic, metaphysics, or mysticism. The universe works according to physical laws that cannot be undone by our pathetic imaginings—and, highly desirable as an afterlife may be to we vainglorious little mortals, a whole cosmosful of parroting adherents doth not a circumventible reality make. As a matter of fact, *it makes no f---ing difference* what one knows, believes, or wants…erase sentience from the picture entirely and the universe will proceed as-is.

So imagine my surprise when I learned there really *is* an Omnipotent, Magnanimous, and All-loving God!

Talk about having Egg on your face!

All my life I'd been disgusted by a perceived intellectual cowardice on the part of virtually every encountered human being, and here I'd suddenly become a fellow babbling weenie.

But, as I said, my soul didn't come easy.

—As to profane images and descriptions—

First, let me make it *amply* clear that God is *not* some silly caricature or phantasmagorical personification! He is most certainly *not* a kindly old man with a long, flowing, snow-white beard. Nor is he plump, rosy-skinned, and obsessed with jollification. In no way does he resemble incendiary shrubbery.

Even attempting to describe Him, in all His Wonderfulness, brings on a play of reverent emotions which absolutely befuddle the process. Already my quill quivers. Console your-selves, then, in knowing you'll find out soon enough...*maybe!*

Now, I realize a lot of this will come off as blasphemous to those of you still adhering to antiquated beliefs. Worse, it will sound like malignant untruth, sick issue, antisocial here-sy...and I offer my apologies in advance. Be all that as it may very well be, it's the truth. Swear to God. It's no fun writing all this down under the pressure of such a mighty Taskmaster, for the sake of a posterity that will no doubt blast it as lies and the ravings of a deranged mind.

So be it.

You opinionated gophers, you oh-so fabulous conform-ists—*you think you know it all!* But you're laboring under an illusion.

You *think* you think.

All your smarmy conclusions are merely worldly wis-dom, and God and I spitteth upon you. Go ahead, hang onto your smug and hypocritical heresies, wallow in your fornicat-ing, sacreligious lifestyles while you can...boy, do you have a comeuppance waiting for you! But I digress.

Your worldly wrongheadedness is really the residue of one of God's early projects. As He explains it, intelligence was something that, like gravity, at first didn't occur to Him, and a truly working brain seemed like so much supercargo on a paradise of a planet where sexual reproduction is a perfect perpetual motion machine. However, intelligence—before The Lord realized how it could backfire—seemed *such* a clever idea. What *would* these creatures do with such a gift? That's what fascinated Him. It was no fun watching the "lower" animals slurp, gallop, and reproduce all day. These new beings couldn't even gallop. They were damned good reproducers, however. Apparently the brain's installation had an unpredicted side-effect: humanity was in heat all year-round. Only one thing to do: leave their played-out carcasses to rot and refurbish the soil, and take the souls, which are very light and compact, and store them up in Heaven. He can't leave our souls "down here" because we are, after all, His children, and you don't keep up a reputation of being Wise, Witty, and Wonderful without a long-term benefits package. But after thousands of years even souls can take up a lot of room, and Heaven's better acreage is already grossly overpopulated. And old souls never die. They just hang around. Naughty ol' Satan, confined as he is to the interior of this embarrassing little rock, has solved the problem. He fries the souls until they resemble crunchy little pork rinds, puts them on a diet of coal dust and bat dung, and makes them listen to Jesse Jackson discourses throughout all eternity. Just for the Hell of it.

—But still the question remains: why *me*?—

Why, out of McBillions of far more likely prospects, did the Good Lord God Almighty pick a stubborn atheist to revise this greatest of books? According to The Lord, there was an unwavering pattern in His interviews, so reliable He considers it a rule: *the feebler the belief, the milder the reaction*, or, inversely, *the more devout the subject, the more hysterical the response*. His past attempts invariably brought on reactions ranging from hysteria to heart attack, making accurate communication impossible. It took The Lord a nerve-wracking night of cajoling, conjuring, and outright bullying to make a believer of me—consequently, when I finally came to my senses and saw The Truth, the typical frenzied reaction was considerably dampened. But at least I was doable—the reaction of all previous candidates was so wild they on the instant became monomaniacal zombies. You're skeptical? Ignore the impotent tracings of my pen. Witness, instead, a planet crawling with visionaries, prophets, and messiahs—all stricken failures of The Lord in His frustrating campaign…and here I sit with my quills, my earplugs, and my Tylenol…quite an honor you think? To be The Lord's personal scribe…but I tell you, the pleasure is most assuredly not mine. The Lord beats a mighty Drum, and I can row only so hard. And His rages are tempestuous, His moods mercurial and infectious. And now another goose-stepping headache is on the way, an all-too familiar sign announcing the Dictater is, once again, getting Impatient. This fate, mine, I wouldn't wish on the lowest sinner, not on the meanest fool.

But it's back to work. Let's see now…

Legerdemainia

—In the beginning—

Right from the start of the Old Bible The Lord has grounds to be upset with humanity's early poor performance at dictation-taking. There *was* no beginning, He points out, and if there had been, it surely would have been His conception that *was* the beginning, for He couldn't have created all this if He Himself hadn't already been in operation, unless of course, He concedes, the original authors meant in the beginning of His activity, which, He notes irritably, would imply a sort of vegetative Deityship activated simply for the future gratification of egotistical little men. "In the beginning," in short, is too vulnerable to misinterpretation, so God has ordered The Book Of Ron to have a better opening; an opening that will more clearly set the pace for what theology is all about:

—Once upon a time God created the heaven and the earth, and
the earth was without form, and void; and darkness *was* upon
the face of the deep—

All this about jumping right to work on this remote hunk of rock really infuriates The Lord. Typical of the mad vanity of our species, to allot our insignificant planet priority in the sequence of universal events. Is it possible that a couple thousand years ago men were so backward? The general tone of the Old Bible is heavily patriarchal, and suggests the pontification of a hard-nosed old Bastard in His mid-fifties given to random acts of sadistic violence, but the mental content of the work brings to mind the poetastry of a bright six year-old with a wild imagination. In actuality, according to God, Earth is one of His more recent projects, and certainly one of His least successful. First on the agenda was some light to see what was going on, and where He was. He recalls "Just sort of floating there" for a "Real long time" with nothing much to do and no one to talk to. Then getting "Kind of paranoid" and wanting to "Do something about it." As anyone who has lived totally alone for an extended period realizes, eventually you get to the point where you begin to vocalize your thoughts.

—And God said, *Let There Be Light*—

He wishes it could have been that easy. In the absolute vacuum of space no sound was generated, for there was no medium to carry waves. But God found that by twirling a Forefinger He was able to create a spiral that generated both heat and light. This first nebula was formed (to give some perspective on our high and mighty attitude toward Earth) so far beyond our present scrutinization of the heavens it will take our technology, even at its headlong pace, another thirty-two thousand years to develop instruments sophisticated enough to breach the gap. Now, one nebula gave plenty of light, but only enough to See that there really wasn't a whole lot *to* see, and that, wherever He was, it was an awfully big place. So God set about hanging new lights, but no matter where He went it was the same old thing. Pretty soon there were star clusters all over, and The Lord, bored almost to inertia, sought to amuse Himself by positioning stars and galaxies to play connect-the-dots. These were whimsical designs: a bowman, a bison, a big or little dipper here and there. Just so were the heavens created; a bit at a time, with patience and great expertise, with insight and, yes, with Love.

But there just didn't seem to be an end to the void, and, since The Lord had eternity on His Hands, He threw Himself into His new hobby with truly deific enthusiasm. After a few billion years it became like a mania, and what was born of simple boredom grew to be a desperate endeavor, a passionate attempt to fill up all this emptiness with enough light to See that there was more emptiness needing light fo fill up the emptiness so He could See there was more emptiness needing light to See the continuing emptiness. Eventually this got to be rather silly and exhausting. There had to be a nobler way to expend the creative energy of what was obviously a very productive and gifted young God, so He got into *detail*. What He had in Mind was some kind of little orbiting system of planetary bodies around one of the lights, a sort of concentric ring-around-the-rosie. Just what shape these satellites should take was an absorbing and delightful puzzle for The Lord in those ages. God became more than a Dabbler in physics. He found that if He zinged a spark just *so* at the light He'd chosen, that spark would whiz around all on its own. He tried it out in lots of places, and had a whale of a time for a few gazillion years, but there becomes a certain routineness to whinging sparks that can grow to be unsatisfying and, even to the Mighty Lord, wearisome.

So it came about that God found Himself plodding lonesomely through endless fields of stars, and thinking what a mess He'd made of the place, and wondering just what the heck there was to do *now*.

And slowly formed a glorious Idea, a scheme for building a little working model of a self-perpetuating environment He'd visualized way back when He was still hanging lights. So gung-ho was The Lord on this new project that he managed to finish it in less than a week.

The first couple of days went into thinking up neat new names for light and darkness and so forth.

God then set about creating a firmament to divide the heaven and earth. This was some fancy Doing. What He Did was part the ocean and sort of flip the firmament into a horizontal position so that half the water was above and half below. Then He moved all the nether water around, exposing land above the seas. He confesses to a certain lapse in Planning here, for He could have saved Himself a lot of Trouble by simply introducing gravity first and allowing the seas to form naturally. The important thing was the thrill of the creative process. God saw that it was Good. But it took all day.

The next step was to give the place a little life and color. He was getting so good at creating He didn't have to use His Hands to whip up any miracles; all He had to do was speak to make it So. He never did quite get the hang of telekinesis…but just by Saying He wanted it—*whoosh*—there were grasses and herbs and fruit-bearing trees everywhere! It was wonderful, it was magic, and boy, was it *Good*. But the details took all day.

The Old, pre-Book Of Ron, Bible is confused here, stating that God now began hanging lights, with the implication that He made earth and grasses and whatnot working blind, and that He *saw* how Good everything *was* in the dark. As I've previously recorded, the sky was already riddled with stars, but God decided His little terrestrial experiment needed a couple lights of its own. So He slapped together a sun and moon, and had a deuce of a time setting them in place. It was dizzying work, making the moon zoom around the earth every twenty-eight days while adjusting the earth to travel in a more stately manner around the sun, then having the sun barely drift through the Milky Way, which was in turn configured to revolve in immense light clusters…but it sure was Good! Yet it took…all…effing…*day*.

The next morning God decided His handiwork could use some locomotion. So He spake into existence whales and fowl, and blessed them and told them to multiply. It was really Good, man, but it *still* took the whole goldurn day.

On the sixth day The Lord, indefatigable as ever, was whale-and fowl watching when it struck Him that there was lots o'planet still to be filled. Whales can make pretty boring pets, and fowl are noisy and smelly at best. Still, the whales got into some interesting antics caused by slow starvation until The Lord *whooshed* some plankton into the seas—one thing led to another, and The Lord just had a ball creating everything that came to Mind. He made cattle and other beasts, and all kinds of creepy things. It's absolutely mind-boggling to imagine the burst of creative Zeal taking place on that sixth day. The number of species on this planet seems almost uncountable, but God was really on a roll. Man, it was *Good*. He designed the thorax, the pulmonary system, the proboscis, the carapace—faster than you can say *whoosh*. Annelids, insectivora, reptiles, amphibians, primates—it was a whirlwind of activity. The platypus, the wombat…then, in a burst of Vanity, something that, in miniature, would resemble Himself. This creature He called man, and this creature He made top dog over the whole earth. Then He kicked back, exhausted. He looked over His experiment and Saw it was *very* Good.

Modesty is, in this instance, a truly deific virtue.

It was spectacular.

—Man alive—

Next day God was totally bushed. He blessed and sanctified the day, but that was about all He felt like getting Into. He was even too tired to make rain, but fortunately a mist that was hanging around warmed, rose, and fell to wet the ground. This little observation got God's creative Spirit back in gear. The damp dust, He found, could be molded into all kinds of shapes, but the one He really liked working on was a male figure. When finished it just lay there, so God decided He'd try to inflate it.

Talk about Finesse!

The Lord's Lips are wider by far than the largest super-galactic cluster, but He managed to blow life into the dust man's nostrils without even shattering it.

Lord God then planted a garden, called the place Eden, and put His little man, spot-named Adam, in charge of all the luscious trees therein. God told Adam to go ahead and eat from any tree save the tree that bore knowledge of good and evil. Lord God was dead-serious about this, and threatened Adam with certain death if he dared, if he essayed, if he even *thought* of disobeying. God, His Wrath resolved, went back to sculpting wet dust, creating a whole neato menagerie to keep Adam company.

But something was still missing. God put Adam to sleep and looked about. There was plenty of dust around to make another person, or even a whole planetful, but Good Old Lord God, prey to a reckless whimsy, decided to fashion this mate from one of Adam's ribs. So He tore open Adam's side, and He *r-r-r-ripped* out a rib. That woke Adam fast enough. Adam lay there howling while The Lord concentrated on the rib, and God admits the howling got on His Nerves and messed up the whole blessed experiment. This new creation was a laughable failure, all rear end and sagging pectorals. Whereas Adam had the potential for strength and prowess and a certain animal cunning, this *Eve* couldn't possibly be good for anything. But, since Adam just gawked at her, The Lord decided to forget all about her for the time being and focus on getting Adam to move around and maybe perform some tricks. Here gravity was the real poser. The Lord, intrigued, inflated Adam a little more and was rewarded by the sight of Adam rising arse-upward into the air, where he hovered like a rag doll with a slack jaw and empty eyes. The Lord putt-putted Adam around for Eve's amusement, but after blankly watching Adam bank and circle for a few minutes she slipped into a heavy sleep. So The Lord dropped Adam and tried to Think of another means of locomotion. There was still a whole lot of space between the ears that wasn't being used for anything, yet God was beginning to develop a strange fascination for Adam's legs. He had, after all, created Adam in His own Image, but He Himself had never encountered a solid surface. He had no Idea what His own Legs were for. Once He managed to stand Adam upright, the little dust man could be prodded along quite nicely. It may seem curious that the idea of a snakewise slither didn't occur to Lord God at that time, but He confesses that slithering gives Him an uneasy Feeling. This Feeling gets validated pretty soon, when a famous snake does something really rotten.

Anyhow, now that things were beginning to take shape, The Great Lord God Almighty looked down with Delight on His creatures and saw they were Good.

And Adam somehow attained the ability to utter his thoughts (which were, understandably, pretty vague) through the unlearned, instantaneous use of speech.

Think of that!

Barely out of the dust stage and he's already putting sentences together.

Not only that, he's taking contol of his environment. He calls Eve "Woman" and acknowledges himself as "Man." Then he's dictating that man and woman should live as husband and wife. This intellectual upstart and his woman—the dust man and the rib lady—were a peripatetic pair, and naked as jays.

—Enter The Snake—

Let this be a lesson to all you silly, irrational, embarrassingly unrealistic Darwinists out there...back when homo sapiens originated, *snakes could already speak as articulately as you and I!*

That's right.

Believe it or not, they were vocal and wily as all get-out.

Nowadays, it's true, snakes haven't gotta whole bunch to say. But back in Edentimes this crafty old viper just slinks right on up to Eve and convinces her to disregard Lord God's edict about avoiding the good and evil tree. The snake tells Eve she and Adam will themselves be gods if they get the inside scoop on good and evil, and won't die at all. The snake was saying, in effect, that The Great and Goodly Lord God Almighty didn't want any competition and so was trying to keep the two in the dark.

So Eve ate of the fruit of the tree and turned Adam on to a piece.

Apparently the fruit caused them to see their nudity as evil, for they were abashed enough to sew aprons out of fig leaves.

But then they heard God's Voice somehow walking in the garden, and had to hide in the trees.

God busted Adam semi-nude.

Adam fessed right up, ashamed as he was with the image of God.

Then, after a quick grilling by The Lord, Adam narked on his mate, setting a precedent for all humanity to come. He fingered Eve, hoping to save his own skin. Eve, catching on quick, pointed her fruit-spattered finger at the snake, who didn't have a finger to point.

God blew it.

He cursed the snake up and down, damned Eve to woeful childbirth, and doomed Adam to hard labor and easy death.

You don't mess with The Great and Goodly Lord God Almighty.

Then God made them suffer the further humiliation of wearing skincoats as He kicked them out of the garden. Realizing the snake was the only genuinely guilty party, The Lord decided to let him hang out, and even *whooshed* in some rather tacky ornamentation—your basic whirling flaming-sword-and-chubby-angels display—to add a little life to the arboretum.

—The Duo Incorrigible—

Once they were out in the real world, the pair went straight from bad to worse. Adam discovered that new people

50

could be produced biologically, which was not only a lot of fun, but a tremendous relief. The last thing he wanted was to lose another rib.

And they named their love child Cain.

Child-making was so much fun the pair got right to work producing another; a boy they named Abel. This Abel grew to be a shepherd, while brother Cain worked the soil.

Eventually the boys decided to get on The Great Lord God's Good Side, so they agreed to bring Him gifts. Abel brought sheep fat, but all Cain could manage was veggies.

Lord God was more than happy with Abel's homage, but fit to be tied over Cain's humble offering. Where was the fat?

Cain was crestfallen.

The boys went into a field and had it out.

When the dust had settled, Abel lay dead and Cain stood vindicated. The phenomenon of sibling rivalry was off to a murderous start.

But God's rage over Abel's death, and over Cain's pathetic gift of all he had, was undiminished. Lord God heaped unbearable punishments upon poor Cain.

Cain was stunned. The Great Good Lord God Almighty had just doomed him to the life of a fugitive and vagabond, with no crops to tend and a price on his head. God then marked Cain for easy assassination, and booted him out into the cold, hard, unforgiving world.

Cain then took a wife, which is pretty strange, since the only woman on the planet was his mom. The oedipal insinuation here is too delicate to broach, but suffice it to say that things began to get a tad on the kinky side, culminating in polygamous doings by Lamech, Cain's great-great-great-great grandson.

—Noah—

Life expectancy was like, *super* high back then. Adam died at 930, while Seth, his third son, lasted until he was 911. Lives this long gave folks the opportunity to reproduce a'plenty; the trend to overpopulation was well on its way.

Lamech was another of the multicentennarian heavy-weights proliferating so widely in those days. He lived to the ripe old age of 777, but sired a boy when he was only 182. This boy—who was to play such an important role in the global shenanigans to follow—young Lamech named Noah, prophesying the boy would comfort humanity, even though The Lord had cursed the ground and was in no mood to parlay.

Now Noah was in his prime, scarcely five centuries old, when Lamech finally passed away, and Noah decided it was time to concentrate on a brood of his own. The result was Shem, Ham, and Japheth (a.k.a. Larry).

Anyway, about this time God's sense of humor was nearing depletion, and He was really sorry He'd ever begun the whole project. So He decided to destroy the works; not only that demented poser man, but the innocent beasts in the fields, the inoffensive winging birds, and all the creepy things. Especially the creepy things.

But God liked Noah. So God gave old Noah ample fore-warning of the Calamity He'd dreamed up, and iterated explicit instructions for building an enormous Ark out of wooden gophers. This was to house not only Noah and his family, but a pair of every living creature on the earth, one male and one female. This was because The Lord, like all artists, couldn't bear to see all His Handiwork destroyed.

Noah was a rather simple fellow, and didn't pause to consider the magnitude of his task, but just got the Mrs. and kids packing and set to work. It took poor Noah almost a hundred years to get the job done, but by the time he was finished he appeared to have aged a thousand years.

He caught malaria and various spotted fevers sweet-talking alligators and king snakes into his clever swamp traps, went half-blind one day luring a squirrel out of a tree, got mauled wrestling a brown bear into captivity. Noah, indeed, was in poor humor after a hundred years of butterfly chasing, grunion hunting, and peeking under various tails. But somehow he got them all together and crammed into the Ark.

What a zoo! As if the stench of the place wasn't bad enough, Noah was soon to discover that hungry tigers and wolves, for instance, don't cohabit well at all with fat yummy ducks, for instance. Also, rabbits and rats and many of the lower animals were very fruitful and *multiplificate*, though not quite so proliferate as the fleas, flies, mites, ticks, tapeworms, and mosquitoes. Giraffes, even in dry dock, were seasick around the clock. Poor Noah's manifest included a hypertensive sloth with the hots for a spider monkey, a hyena with insomnia, and a Tasmanian Devil whose idea of a good time was to sneak up and scare the daylights out of him.

For a whole week the Ark remained grounded while The Lord aggregated hydrogen and oxygen molecules into a great liquid atmosphere. Making rain is no quick trick, and God was beginning to Think it would be just as tough to destroy life as create it, when the seventh day passed and the deluge began.

—Captain Noah—

For forty days and forty nights it rained cats and dogs, and everybody was perfectly miserable, what with the cold and damp and the howling and braying. Noah, who was a ripe 600 years old, suffered through the constant sniffling and aching joints with the quiet humility of a willing dupe.

And still it rained. And rained and rained. The sodden Ark was borne up and drifted out on the face of the waters; up, up, fully fifteen cubits above the land. Naturally, every living thing on dwindling terra was exterminated, and for weeks the water was littered with the carnage of fowl and cattle and creepy things. But old Noah and his brood just drifted on, week after week, month after month, futilely searching the horizon while resolutely accepting their dreary fate.

Meanwhile The Lord was busy hanging new lights in the firmament of the heavens, amusing Himself by flicking away bits of energy to create comets, playing a sort of cosmic tiddly-winks with galactic matter.

After tooling around the heavens for a few months He remembered Noah and Co. bobbing around down here, so He turned off the tap and blew away the clouds to see if anything was left.

Sure enough, there was Noah, soaked to the bone and still scraping the Ark's rank mushy deck; a creaky old codger given to mumbling and grumbling and the scratching of imaginary bites.

The Lord got busy right away, but it took Him over ten months to blot up most of the mess. The Ark got stuck on Mount Ararat when the earth finally dried to its present paradisical state.

—God Makes An Announcement—

Seeing His work *was* Good, The Lord told everybody to pile out and multiply.

And the entire menagerie wobbled, pitched, and staggered off the Ark, old Noah and his dung-crusted spade dragging the rear.

Noah, half-crazed, built an altar to God, then flipped out completely. He ran amok with his spade and barrow, slaughtering the clean beasts and fowl and barbecuing them on the altar.

"That does it," said The Lord. "Here I'm stuck with nothing but dirty beasts and some old nut who's a pain in the Holy Neck. But I can See what good it does trying to straighten things out. This time," vowed the Great and All-forgiving God Almighty, "I won't curse the ground or pick on these puny living things. Noah, I bless you and your boys and grant you the right to eat anything you want, excluding relatives."

With The Lord's blessing, Shem, Ham, and Larry took their wives to town and started bonking like crazy.

—Noah Ties One On—

Meanwhile Noah, with time on his hands and grieving his lost occupation, husbanded the first vineyard. He mastered the art of wine-making and whooped it up by himself in his tent all night. There is some uncertainty about Noah's activities during that night-long bacchanalia, but in the morning a shocked Ham found his father naked and out like a light. Shem and Larry then put a cloak over their father, for a buck-naked 601 years-old man in a drunken coma is not a pretty sight. Noah woke hungover and in a terrible mood. Since Canannan, his grandchild by Ham, had absolutely nothing to do with covering him up and enraging him so, Noah put a curse on the boy and doomed him to familial servitude. The Lord was delighted to see that old Noah still had his sense of humor, and left him alone in his tent with his booze and his funky spade. The common ancestor of all winos, Noah clung to his shattered existence for another 350 years, finally passing away in withered, sniveling ignominy.

—The Plot Sickens—

The generations passed rapidly, and it became pretty obvious that man was here to stay. Already he could postulate sillily, dance like the dickens, and carry on rudimentary conversations. And boy, could he come up with some wild names for his kids! Some of Larry's children were stuck with real doozies, like *Magog, Dodanim, Ashkenaz, and Togarmah*—Yeah!—while Ham, not to be outdone, was responsible for beauties such as *Phut, Cush*, and *Mizraim* (and of course poor *Canannan*, the family fall guy), and indirectly responsible for gems like *Asshur* and *Rehoboth*.

—SRO—

Now, coprolalia is no laughing matter, but in practically no time the whole planet was inundated, and this phonetic awkwardness had evolved to a fine art. And everybody journeyed to the east and settled in Shinar.

Why?

That old, obsolete Bible doesn't tell us why, but The Great And Marvelous Lord God Almighty demands it be noted in The Book Of Ron that, when He sincerely tried to fine tune the aimlessly milling multitude in Shinar, everybody at noon abruptly stopped and said to one another in unison: *"Go to, let us make brick and burn them thoroughly."* God wanted to be sick.

And everybody suddenly had the same bright idea: they would build a tower to heaven, which was a mere 205,000[655] light years distant. God came down to check out this latest act of mortal lunacy and, Almightily embarrassed, scattered 'em all right back out of Shinar and splintered their common language.

—One More Try—

Now, it's true that everybody so far had turned out to be a holy flop, but The Lord was a Diehard at Heart, and firm in His belief that *someone* out there wasn't beyond help. So it was that, after glumly watching a few more generations of humans breed, The Lord started looking about for a ripe pigeon. He picked Abram, son of Terah, and promised him celebrity and protection if he would only ditch his family, country, and home.

That all sounded pretty good to Abram. So Abram took his nephew Lot and his shapely wife Sarai and they headed for Canaan.

In Canaan Abram built an altar to God, then traveled to a mountain east of Bethel, where he built another. Abram had the situation pegged. The Lord was crazy about altars. Sensing he was on a roll, Abram continued south, but ran into a famine which forced him to cool it on the altar-building and head for Egypt.

This posed a huge problem for wayfaring Abram.

He was about to confront one of the great trials that hit men who marry for looks.

You see, Sarai was a real corker. And Abram was hip enough to the Egyptian brand of testosterone to realize that, once they got a gander, his goose would be cooked.

Abram managed to pass off sweet Sarai as his sister, which meant Pharaoh could get his greasy elite paws on her common luscious beauties without having to disembowel wily egocentric Abram first. The plan worked out *perfectly*. Abram got the royal treatment in exchange for his toots: servants, sheep, oxen, and even asses!

The sly old fox! He comes into Egypt a vagabond, pawns off his hot little honey to the high muckety-muck, and next thing you know he's related to the richest guy in town. Lord knows, literally speaking, which of the many feminine plagues lovely Sarai brought upon the house of Pharaoh, but

Pharaoh did what any obscenely rich guy would do and sent her packing, Abram and Lot in tow.

—The Continuing Adventures Of Abram—

Now Abram was *loaded*. He'd come out of the Egyptian affair a rich man; with cattle, with gold and silver.

He, Lot, and the oh-so comely Sarai returned to Abram's mountain altar.

Both Abram and Lot had so many tents, flocks, and herds that there wasn't enough land to support them all, which caused their respective herdsmen to have a falling-out. Abram and Lot decided to divvy the place up between them—Lot taking the Sodom side and Abram taking the Canaan side.

Abram knew which side his bread was buttered on.

Seeing a touch of mortal competition, he wasted no time. He settled in the plain of Mamre and built an altar *pronto*.

—Slimepits And Shoelatchets—

Worse even than to want is to have. Abram was finding out that, just as the Egyptians coveted Sarai's gorgeous goodies, so his new neighbors had an eye on his garish goods. Smiters smote, folks got carried away, arrogant little humans set precedents everywhere. After the dust had settled, Abram was richer than ever and the friend of kings. God was certainly making good on His end of the deal.

—After The Lovin'—

But time was catching up with Abram, who now found himself in the grip of some pretty wild hallucinations. He went star-tripping with God, Who, ever the Showman, got off on tearing live animals in half for His and Abram's amusement. This went on all day long until the night came and Abram crashed, for some reason paranoid of the dark. SomeBody must have slipped him Something. He dreamt of God talking to him about what great good buddies they were, and about all the blessings that were to come to the progeny of God's favorite little altar builder. Abram woke to more hallucinations, this time to some supercreepy visions of smoking furnaces and burning lamps. He was in no mood for altars.

—The Old And The Restless—

Things were swinging in the house of Abram. With Sarai's blessing he got it on with her Egyptian handmaid Hagar. Everybody got bent out of shape when Hagar got knocked up, and Hagar felt horrible. She took off into the wilderness. So Good Old God of course put a curse on her. It was a doozie. Hagar was doomed to perpetual childbirth and to submission to kinky Sarai. So it came to pass that, at the age of 86, virile but burnt-out Abram had Hagar bear him a wild young boy. This was Ishmael.

—The Agony And The Agony—

Thirteen years passed.

Now Abram, even though he was only 99, was no spring chicken. He tended to laugh at inappropriate times, and was constantly falling on his face. God was not amused. He made poor Abram walk in front of Him, demanding perfection every step of the way. But down went Abram again, flat on his face. The Lord took umbrage. There was just no way to get the bugs out of these recalcitrant little humans, no matter how hard you trained them, no matter how well they were rewarded. So God decided to make an example of Abram. He picked him up and dusted him off, renamed him Abraham, and cursed the old man into stud service. Abraham just laughed and fell on his face. God's rage was Immense, but His sense of Humor was indomitable. He had to come up with something really, really, *really* good. And He did! He decided—now get this—to order every boy be—it's difficult to be delicate here—every boy have his…that is to say, have his member, if you can believe it…*sliced away around the head!* Old Abraham just fell on his face, laughing insanely. But he wasn't so senile he didn't fear The Great And Kindly Lord's wrath. Abraham got his blade and went to town, slicing like the Devil was after him. He even went under the knife himself. These were some pretty gory times, and God was pleased.

—XXX—

Incest, drunkenness, and a general good time were had by all. Sarai, renamed Sarah, caught Abraham's laughing disease, but was still canny enough to appreciate the power of denial. The couple were now senior citizens, and Abraham was way too far gone to fulfill God's stud curse. He did, however, love his wine. So The Lord sent a couple of Lot's horny daughters into Abraham's tent to get him wasted and laid and give Sarah a giggle or two. I won't go into details (you can read it yourself!) but, man, those were the days.

—The Sucker Trade—

Abraham now pulled the old Pharaoh trick again. He went south and passed Sarah off as his sister to king Abimelech (no kidding) of Gerar (no kidding!). Even though the king didn't score, cunning Abraham got sheep, oxen, a thousand pieces of silver, servants, *and* Sarah back! You don't have to teach an old dog new tricks.

—Gall In The Family—

At an even 100 years old, with a little help from God, Sarah birthed another boy, named Isaac, by Abraham. Eight days later, slipping in and out of reality, old Abe pulled out his trusty mutilation knife and got to business while Sarah watched, shrieking with hilarity. But she stopped laughing soon enough. Once little Isaac was weaned, he began mocking her for not being his true mom; Isaac, you'll remember, was a product of Abe's and Hagar's whoopee-making. Sarah, seeing red, made Abraham kick out Hagar and their love child. Fearing he'd be seen as a bad provider, Abraham rummaged through all his gold and silver and masses of wealth, finally settling on good old, practical bread and water. He heaped kid, bread, and water on poor Hagar's shoulders, and kicked her out into the wilderness.

Legerdemainia

—The Ghoulies—

Sarah finally died at well over a hundred; Abe hung on until the big one-seven-five. Even so, after he'd buried Sarah, he still had enough in him to remarry and sire six more kids! When at last he croaked, Isaac and brother Ishmael buried him in a cave, then dug him up and buried him in a field next to Sarah.

The gazillion-year spate of boredom was irrevocably dissolved: God had created an insane and irrepressibly horny playground for generations to come. He foresaw cell phones and low riders, televangelists and garage bands, tailgate jocks and shamelessly-public pregnant soccer moms in spandex and heels. Fatcats and posers and pop stars and pinheads and oh God, oh God, was it ever Goo-oo-*ood!*

—Thus Endeth The Book Of Ron—

He hath an almighty headache, and his Merciful God doth grant him a break. So he riseth now, layeth down his quill, and slammeth shut The goddamn Book Of Ron. Unto The Lord's people he goeth, that they may worship his Master's Word. Fall flat on thine faces, ye sheep, and bless yourselves, your loved ones, and the innumerable sons of all your crucifix-hawkers to be: it can only get deeper, for the slaughterhouse is boundless, the worm is on the rise, and our Wise, Witty, and Wonderful Shepherd hath all the time in the world.

A Deeper Cut

Devon passed out.

That's what they told him, anyway.

He'd been waiting in line like everyone else, and next thing he knew he was the center of attention for a ring of bystanders, a pair of old ladies were rubbing his arms, and the bank manager was asking if he needed an ambulance.

The worst part, initially, was the embarrassment. But on the drive home an icy fear crimped the back of his neck, made his shoulders lock up and his elbows seize, made his hands sweat all over the wheel. What if it happened again? What if it happened while driving? He could be barreling along nicely, completely absorbed in the intricacies of lane surfing, and— BAM: dead man. Or find he'd unconsciously plowed though a crosswalk full of horrified lunchtime toddlers. Splattered innocence, crippled joy. The image was so appalling Devon had a phantom episode, imagining, in one missed heartbeat, that he'd blacked out again, and was surfacing anew.

He pulled over with excessive caution; using only the rear-view mirror lest, in looking back for even a moment, some inexplicable mini-seizure should send him hurtling into a compound bloody fireball. Perspiration bathed his face and chest. He'd always been the healthiest of men; didn't drink, didn't touch drugs, didn't over-exert. Gradually the tremors passed. But not the terror; it was a vital shadow in the center of his skull. Devon called a cab and a tow truck. He sat slumped in the back of the cab, drawing faux calm around him like a horsehair shroud. The driver was a talker; Devon let him roll on. All he could see was the cab's windshield, streaked and bespattered, a broken mosaic of shocked baby faces that never had a chance to grow.

"Your scans are clean," Dr. Goodman beamed. The clipboard, facing away, would not elaborate. "I think we can cheerfully write off the cause of this visit as one of those little anomalies that pop into our lives, shake us up a bit to give our egos some perspective, and then pop right back out as though nothing occurred. And who knows? Maybe nothing did. Sometimes nature just drops the ball for no apparent reason. I like to compare the body to a complex harp with one or more strings always out of tune, and hard work and healthful living as the elements that retune those—Mr. Devon?"

Devon blinked at him. A low hum had just passed through his brain like a train through a tunnel. There were things in there, moving around, clattering without sound. It was as if his thoughts were loose shingles on a roof, responding to a sudden high wind. He blew over.

Devon opened his eyes to another perspective. It was a skewed view, of three vulnerable specimens frozen in a brightly lit box. The action resumed: receptionist slipping out of room, staring strangely over shoulder, doctor frowning at clipboard, planted squarely before seated patient.

Goodman's entire demeanor had changed. He tapped his pencil on the clipboard—*thuda-thuda-thud*—little alien heartbeats in rubber on pressed cork. "You've heard of narcolepsy, Mr. Devon? Once we've ruled out the obvious— epilepsy, tumor, arrhythmia—we have to rely on conjecture, which, in a mature practice, comes down to empiricism rather than guesswork. What I'm trying to say is: symptoms are templates. Narcolepsy is a known condition, but it's not a common one. I'm not going to beat around the bush here. In narcolepsy, the brain's steady-state waking electrical activity is abruptly interrupted—the subject goes to sleep on the spot, rather than drifting away naturally. Why? The current's been cut off, the lights shut down. *Why?* We don't know yet; and there's that dreadful non-answer which seems, to the anxious layperson, an evasion rather than a helpful response. But it's all we've got. That, and a medication I'm prescribing. Don't worry about the endless string of Latin syllables. Although still in the experimental stage, it shows tremendous promise in the short-term. However, there's a caveat: you must be prudent in your approach to everyday activities whenever a recurrence might prove injurious to yourself or to others, and you must curtail these activities any time you experience symptoms that are in any way out of the ordin—"

"Mr. Devon?" Goodman's smile was frayed around the edges. "Are you feeling all right now? We were discussing your prescription when you appear to have remissed momentarily. I've checked your vitals and you're good as gold. The episode was very brief, yet it absolutely confirms my immediate diagnosis of narcolepsy." He nervously drummed his fingers on the clipboard. "Miss Aines is going to administer a single dose of your prescription, and you are thereafter not to approach the medication without my approval over the phone. As I said, it's experimental, but entirely safe. Then I want you to go home and take a load off—a load off your mind as well as your feet. I'd prefer you walk rather than use a cab or bus. Moderate exercise is always a precursor to healthful recovery." He pulled open the door, hesitating halfway. "If you experience a recurrence, or become morbidly anxious, or entertain any weird, traumatic sense of alienation, I want you to give me a call right away. Miss Aines will produce my home and cell numbers as soon as you've received your medication and taken that single dose." He smiled genially while ushering Devon out. "I know you're going to be just fine."

Strangest thing.

How can a man *know* what's going on around him, behind him, within him—when he can't see or feel a thing? Devon was unconscious. The infinitesimally vague electrical discharges were unlike anything he'd ever experienced, so he had no point of reference, but he *knew* his brainwaves were somehow being manipulated—by somebody or something from somewhere bleak and far away—for reasons of cold research, for inhuman experiment, for purposes that made no sense whatever in regular terms. He could tell, by focusing, that a kind of frustrated enmity pervaded the ether connecting whoever he was with whatever they were, and that if he let go for even a second they'd—

"Sir?" A thumb peeled back Devon's eyelid. Sensible impressions were returning. The sounds of traffic. The inside of a paramedics' van, seen gurney-up. A man's face; a face like any other. "Sir, can you feel the pressure of my hand on your arm?" A pinching above the elbow. "How about now?" The full-screen thumb splintered into five fingers on a rocking hand. "Follow my hand with your eyes, sir." The face turned. "He's receptive." The face turned back. "You're in an ambulance, Mr. Devon. We're taking you to the emergency room at Mother Of Mercy Hospital. But we've determined this is no emergency; that's why we're not using the siren. So just relax; what's going on is purely procedural. You appear to have blacked out while sitting on the bus bench at White and Lincoln, yet no one observed any evidence of seizure or foul play. There's no indication of brain trauma, no signs of physical injury, and all your responses to outside stimuli are well within the normal range. Do you feel okay now?"

Devon's voice phased in and out. "Yes, I'm fine. I just need to—"

Two strong hands gripped his biceps. "You'll have to remain quiet, sir. Until you've been thoroughly examined you're under our supervision. It won't be long. There's the hospital now. We're pulling up to emergency. Try to stay calm."

"I can't be strapped down. That's what they want." Devon's mouth was too dry for more.

The paramedic rattled a prescription bottle. "The label reads fifty. The count is forty-nine. I'd call yours a pretty extreme reaction. Now just relax."

The van stopped with the gentlest jolt. A moment later the rear doors swung open, and the paramedic said, softly, "You're under restraint only for your own safety, okay? We can't have you blacking out and rolling off the gurney now, can we, Mr. Devon?"

A hydraulic whine, a rocking and settling. A new voice said, "Okay to roll."

The bright assault of antiseptic fluorescence made Devon's eyes burn. Faces looked on curiously as he was wheeled by; faces as indifferent as the paramedic's, as indifferent as Dr. Goodman's, as indifferent as that burned-out receptionist behind the glass, as—

The electrical activity, Devon realized, functioned incidentally as a conduit. They were getting into his head, and they were learning what it means to be human, but it was hard work. Through this connection he'd become electrically empathic—able to glean their drive and exasperation, to know that, through their resolution, they *were going to learn* what they needed, if they didn't kill him in the process, or if he was unable to kill himself first. He was experiencing their excitement as well as their frustration, their urgency and their demand. He was losing hold, losing self-control. He knew it. He could feel it.

"Well, I'm taking him *off* the medication, at least for the present, and I don't give a good holy crap what you or Lancet have to say on the matter, is that clear enough for you? As of right now he's under our care. Your prescription arguably precipitated this patient's arrival, and there's absolutely no reason to believe it's mitigating his condition in the least. Fine. You can talk to the coordinator in the morning. I'm presently handling Mr. Devon, and this conversation is officially concluded. Now go back to sleep!"

Devon embraced the room's hard white light like a lover. He kept his eyes fixed wide, afraid to even blink, as Dr.

Grant firmly replaced the receiver and turned, hands clasped behind his back.

"Mr. Devon, you're doing great. You've been through a bit of a scare, but there's no reason to worry. Your provider has authorized any necessary procedures, though I'm confident we've no cause for alarm." He raised Devon's prescription bottle like a dead lizard. "As of this moment you're off these. I'm going to give you a sedative to help you relax. We're calling a cab. I want you to go home and get some sleep. You have an appointment with Dr. Randall for Thursday at nine."

"No, please…give me something that'll help me stay awake. They're getting closer. If I fall asleep they'll be right back in."

Dr. Grant stood quietly, his expression sour. "Who's getting closer?"

Facets of his identity were falling like flakes of dand-ruff. Memories were being stripped, copied, filed; Devon's humanness was being assaulted, weakness by weakness. The excitement was palpable; he was naked, he was down, he was roadkill. His flaws were being recognized and categorized, in some universal way only a natural predator could understand. Humans were easy, they were fait accompli. Devon could struggle all he wanted, but he was pinned and purpling, a pretty bruised butterfly. He thrashed, but didn't budge, called, but didn't peep, screamed—

"The more you fight me," snarled the security guard, "the harder I fight back. You *got* that?" He shoved Devon into a plastic chair, one of many lined against the wall.

"Listen to me!" Devon begged. "I can't hold on any longer. Please. Something."

The guard sneered over his shoulder. "*I'll* give you something." He pressed the intercom's call button. "Security on floor one, east wing. I have a disturbed patient who somehow got out into the hall. Not a biggie, but Riley and Forbes, I'd like you to assist."

The feelers were in. He was going. A great company was in his skull; a kind of delirious clamor and buzzing crescendo. Devon was a transparent display, every nerve-ending under intense scrutiny. Ecstasy, comprehension, anticipation. His mind was being peeled open; his nightmares, his mistrust, his mortal horror.

Devon leaped from his chair, tore the guard's gun from its holster, crammed the barrel in his mouth. A bear-hug and shattering of teeth. The gun went spinning across the floor. There was a hard stomping down the hall, a flurry of shouts, the pulsing buzz of an alarm.

He was seizing. His arms were shaking wildly, his eyes bursting from their sockets. Liquid fire tore through his frame, spewed from his mouth and nostrils, set his fraying hair ablaze.

Devon hit the plate glass window like a bug smacking into a windshield. He blew out into the night, a mass of porcupine shards, blood spraying in his wake. He heard Dr. Grant puffing behind. "Mr. Devon! Stop! For the love of God! *Stop!*"

He was rocking madly, his skin blistering, his organs swelling to bursting. Devon's head snapped back and his mouth ripped at the corners, peeled off his face and blew away in shreds. His ribcage shattered from the sternum down. He was being zipped open, torn apart, dug into. With a shriek of bone his spine snapped free, his pelvis collapsed, his skull halved to expose the hysterical animal writhing within.

"Mr. Devon! Somebody call the gate. Devon!"

Devon's brain turned to cartilage, to sponge, to jelly. The cerebellum split, the cortex gave way, and they were in. Electrical energy; frying, probing, hurtling into every cell.

"Mr. Devon!"

Night sucked him up like a giant straw. Consciousness was a black and wiggly thing, all-feeding, all-absorbing, all-encompassing, all

"*De—*

Victorious

Scotty Skatbord hauled his head out of the dumpster, his bleached-blond locks wagging. "Two cans and a plastic litre!"

"*Awe*some!" Sackageegaws handed the treasures to Suki, who placed them neatly in her heavy-duty garbage bag.

"No, *bi*-och!" Eye Bee plucked out the items and flattened them with monster stomps. "How many time I gots to tell you? Make…*space!*"

Roach shuddered, staring up at the night. "Space…" He looked back down. "And how many times *you* gotta be told, homey, to *not* use *that* word?"

Eye Bee nodded grimly and showed his fist. The Klee-shaes all matched the gesture, extending their arms until knuckles met in the gang's secret street salute.

"To kicking greenman butt!" Roach vowed.

"Hallelujah!" Sackageegaws breathed.

Eye Bee stopped dead. "Say *what?*"

Sackageegaws bristled. "It's a sacred term. One my people used to fight off the damn Pilgrims, okay? Suddenly *you* don't know all about prejudice?"

Suki stepped between them. "Come on, you two! We not lose sight what we fight for!"

"Against," Scotty amended.

"What*ever*. Klee-shae a unit, baby, and we never forget that, or we lose before begin."

"Right on!"

The Klee-shaes punched fists again. Their gang name was an amalgam: "Klee" from a popular brand of tissue, and "shae" from a New York baseball stadium now being used as an arms warehouse in the Fartian War. Since Kleenex®, the tissue named, was used for nose-blowing and wiping up residue, the gang's credo proclaimed: *We gonna blow away the greenman like the snot he be, wipe him to da moon and back, and trow his funky little space ass in da trash where it belong!* The Klee-shaes were not to be confused with Da Branededz, a loose assemblage of peripatetic Christian proselytizers, or the Starry o'Types, a Mickey's-swilling conglomerate of steel drummers and bongoheads—all ex-rival gangs, now united in the common war against the despised Fartians.

"Jam!" Scotty swore. "How we supposed to fight those radical little dudes with these pickings?" He raised a plastic 12-ounce Coke bottle in either hand.

"Sometime," grated Suki, stamping a foot, "I just get *so* anger! Fartiaman give us two thousand buck a month, some cheap-ass condo, and a crapload of food stamp ain't no good whatever on street. How we suppose to meet cost of living? When we gonna get another raise? This terrorism bo-sheet gotta end. It *gonna* end!"

Roach drop-kicked a trash can. "They want us soft, homegirl! Don't you get it? That's why they give us so much—so we'll get lazy and won't be able to fight back."

"Klee-*shaes*," Eye Bee proclaimed, "ain't soft! And Ichabod Bartholemew Tawkins ain't about to lay down fo no alien hijink. You all stiff?"

"We stiff!"

"Then let's do it!"

"I'm with ya, dog!"

"Mazel tov!"

"We ready!"

"Far out, dude!"

And with that the real war, the war of the streets, was on. The Klee-shaes splintered on Main and reconnoitered at Minor, bivouaced on Major and surfaced at Admiral. This was no haphazard assault: they'd group-fantasized overthrowing the Fartian's Earthfare complex countless times. The grounds surrounding the complex extended a good square mile. It looked like Woodstock—if Woodstock had been lit by a vast ring of streetlamps, peppered with carnival rides, daycare centers, and concession stands, and littered with over three thousand porta-potty outhouses, most used as living quarters by homeless and substance-dependent terrans; silently suffering soldiers in the guts-and-glory war with the Fartians.

The Klee-shaes pimp-strutted purposefully up the long walk leading to the building's main entrance, their cylinders a'clickin'. Veterans of ease flashed their bedsores and plaque, mothers of war raised their fat children high. This was it; the real thing. Men poured along the Klee-shaes' flanks, chanting "Oof-oof-oof!" in the manner of Cheetos®-snarfing Rose Bowlers, women shook their moons and udders hysterically. As they approached the steps the Klee-shaes could hear a terran favorite over the great building's Public Address system—it was Neil Young warbling *Keep On Rocking In The Free World*, but a Fartian host, misunderstanding the moment, transferred the track to Mollify. Instantly The Boss was belting it out, right on cue and *over* and *over* and *over* and— "*Bohn* in da USA! *Bohn* in da USA!" The mob went gablivaschnocketyboogle. Klee-shaes vaulted the steps and kicked in the doors, stormed down the main hall demolishing anything green. The huge lobby was socked in, but the crowd intuitively cleared a path: this was serious business, baby; this was genuine Earth business at last.

The tension produced a drug-like euphoria as the Klee-shaes stomped across the lobby. Eye Bee acknowledged his familiars with macho nods and glares: there were Logy and Wheezil, Sfinkter and Lee Mur, Stickypawz, Shrieking Violet, Gangho and Boilpuss. In Eye Bee's camouflage pockets waited a cattle prod and brass knuckles. Maybe it was time to spill a little funky green blood.

Their Fartian smiled politely upon opening the door. "How may I please you?"

"You can start," Eye Bee hissed, "by kissing my shiny black ass."

The Fartian blushed kelly green. "Forgive me, special sir, but there are moral considerations—"

Suki restrained Eye Bee with a steadier arm. "Enough with make stalling, you little poof. How come my TV don't get no freaking satellite?"

The Fartian hopped about nervously. "But my dear, it was most necessary to ground those satellites. They were emitting gamma—"

Roach showed a threatening fist. "Gamma, yo mama!" Cheers rang in the lobby.

The Fartian looked like he would faint. "Counselor YoMama is currently unavailable, sirs and madams. An accident in Charity Center. Apparently YoMama's face encountered a flurry of anxious clients. He is in Recovery, and will be back in service with manifold apologies."

Roach rammed him aside. "They ain't gonna be no recovery, slimeboy. Where you hide your head honcho?"

"Sir?"

"The Jolly Green Giant, you quivering turd! You know *just* who I'm rapping about."

"I...I..."

Sackageegaws stepped in. "Back off, Roach. This here situation calls for a woman's touch." She rubbed the Fartian's trembling round crown. "What's your name, sweetheart? What do they call you?"

"Terrans," the Fartian managed, "have generously honored me with the lovely appellation 'DieBitch', which I graciously respond to whenev—"

Suki threw him into a headlock, a fist pressed against his nasal apertures. "I gonna show you woman touch! Now you listen up, *Die*-Beech. We Earthman ain't gonna take no more of this bo-sheet, y'hear? So you gonna take us to your leader, *right now*, you gots me, or we gonna smash you into gooey little pile of kiwi jam."

Eye Bee pulled out his brass knuckles.

Their Fartian squirmed free of the headlock and slapped his sissy-ass flippers against his cheeks. Scotty rode circles around the knot of Klee-shaes as their prisoner was cattle-prodded across the floor and into a huge storeroom. Here an elderly Fartian, no less wimpy than DieBitch, was meticulously ordering parcel allocations—shelves were overflowing with returned televisions, blenders, stereos, and microwaves. Over-sized tags could be seen hanging from the articles, with labels reading: WRONG   COLOR,   LOUD   TIMER,   STICKY BUTTON, etc.

Eye Bee didn't waste time on introductions. He marched straight up to the head Fartian and knuckle-dusted him right in his just-begging-for-it face. "That's for Earth!" Whoops rang in the lobby. It was obvious mustered terrans were reappropriating their beloved planet.

Roach scooped him off the floor, slapped him once for good measure, and sat him back in his chair.

"Now you gonna listen to the Klee-shaes, you little booger, and you gonna let the whole damn human race know we means business. You gonna put us up on that..." He snapped his fingers. "...on that..."

"Times Square screen!" blurted Scotty.

"That's the one! Just like the Klee-shaes planned." Roach shoved Scotty forward. "You tell him. And make him knows we stiff."

"No bo-sheet!" said Suki.

"Jam, dude!" Scotty got right in the First Fartian's swollen gushing face. "We're up for a hairy 360, you radical little hodad dude, and it's like you're airborne if you're not totally awesome, you dig?"

"No *bo-sheet!*"

Eye Bee zapped him with the cattle prod. The First squealed and slapped his flippers against his newly-indented face.

"Do him again," grated Sackageegaws. This time the First yelped and leaped from his chair.

Roach shoved him right back down. "Klee-shaes knows you can do it, cause you done it befo'." He looked around. "And you done it from right here, in this very room. I recognizes it.

This is where you announced all that free chocolate peanut butter toffee ice cream."

Sackageegaws grabbed the First by his pencil-thin neck. Her eyes were blazing. "I gained six pounds offa that damned ice cream!"

Eye Bee meaningfully smacked the brass knuckles against his palm. "Move it, fart-boy, or we gonna do a little Rambo dance on your pussy green head."

The First pressed a button under his desk. A video camera dropped from a ceiling recess, and a wall panel rolled aside to reveal a 6 x 4 screen. A red light came on below the camera's lens. The First appeared onscreen, surrounded by quickly repositioned Klee-shaes. He pushed another button and gagged, "Thank you so much. You may now speak."

"Yo yo yo," called Eye Bee. "Lissen up, peeps of Earth. We is I.B. Tawkins, Roach Arroyo, Suki Kukinuki, Scotty Skatbord, and Jusplain Sackageegaws. We is the Klee-shaes, baby, here to say we done taked back the planet!"

"No bo-sheet!"

"Right on!"

"Gnarly, dude!"

"Top o' the mornin'!"

An insert appeared in the screen's right-hand corner, showing the Square in real time. It looked like V-Day. Folks were leaping, handguns blazing, sailors necking with...well, *sailors*.

"Now," Eye Bee said, "for a little payback." He began pulling merchandise off the shelves. "Where you keep the big screens and the high defs?"

"It just like Fartiaman," Suki fumed. "Hide alla good stuff."

"My people," grunted Sackageegaws, "have suffered long enough." She and Scotty tore open the tall doors leading to a closet containing control panels for the Fartian vessel chargers. They staggered back out dragging masses of insulated cable.

"Come *on!*" Roach snapped. "What we gonna get for all that space jive?"

"Jam!" Scotty said, shaking his head. "It's *copper!*"

This has been only one story, of many heroes. What's important is the Fartian War is history.

The extrastellar menace is behind us.

We can all rest easy knowing our children are secure, our ethos reborn, our constitutions intact. One future day another invader may make the mistake of testing our God-given will. Let this record be a warning; a warning sent gloriously streaming into the cold alien depths—encased in an *Earthling* space capsule, shot from an *Earthling* launch pad, and with a very *Earthling* caveat:

DO—*NOT*—MESS—WITH—*EARTH!*

Punk.